Montgomery City Public Library
Montgomery City, MO

P9-DGR-025

# CODE TALKER

A Novel About the Navajo Marines of World War Two

JOSEPH BRUCHAC

Dial Books  New York

DIAL BOOKS
A member of Penguin Group (USA) Inc.
Published by The Penguin Group
Penguin Group (USA) Inc., 375 Hudson Street, New York, NY 10014, U.S.A.
Penguin Group (Canada), 10 Alcorn Avenue, Toronto, Ontario, Canada M4V 3B2
(a division of Pearson Penguin Canada Inc.)
Penguin Books Ltd, 80 Strand, London WC2R 0RL, England
Penguin Ireland, 25 St. Stephen's Green, Dublin 2, Ireland
(a division of Penguin Books Ltd)
Penguin Group (Australia), 250 Camberwell Road, Camberwell, Victoria 3124,
Australia (a division of Pearson Australia Group Pty Ltd)
Penguin Books India Pvt Ltd, 11 Community Centre, Panchsheel Park,
New Delhi - 110 017, India
Penguin Group (NZ), Cnr Airborne and Rosedale Roads, Albany, Auckland 1310,
New Zealand (a division of Pearson New Zealand Ltd)
Penguin Books (South Africa) (Pty) Ltd, 24 Sturdee Avenue, Rosebank,
Johannesburg 2196, South Africa
Penguin Books Ltd, Registered Offices: 80 Strand, London WC2R 0RL, England

Copyright © 2005 by Joseph Bruchac
All rights reserved
Designed by Jasmin Rubero
Text set in Adobe Caslon
Printed in the U.S.A. on acid-free paper

20  19  18  17  16  15  14  13

Library of Congress Cataloging-in-Publication Data
Bruchac, Joseph, date.
Code talker : a novel about the Navajo Marines of World War Two /
Joseph Bruchac.
p.   cm.
Summary: After being taught in a boarding school
run by whites that Navajo is a useless language, Ned Begay
and other Navajo men are recruited by the Marines to become
code talkers, sending messages during World War II in their
native tongue.
ISBN 0-8037-2921-9
[1. Navajo language—Fiction. 2. Cryptography—Fiction. 3. Navajo
Indians—Fiction. 4. Indians of North America—Southwest,
New—Fiction. 5. United States. Marine Corps—Indian troops—Fiction.
6. World War, 1939–1945—Fiction.]
I. Title.
PZ7.B82816Co 2005
[Fic]—dc22
2003022792

43360

This book is dedicated
to those who have always,
in proportion to their population,
volunteered in the greatest numbers,
suffered the most casualties,
won the most Purple Hearts
and decorations for valor,
and served loyally
in every war fought by the
United States against foreign enemies,
from the American Revolution
to Afghanistan and Iraq—
to the American Indian soldier.

974-15 Brf 89.73

# CONTENTS

# CODE TALKER

# Listen, My Grandchildren

Grandchildren, you asked me about this medal of mine. There is much to be said about it. This small piece of metal holds a story that I was not allowed to speak for many winters. It is the true story of how Navajo Marines helped America win a great war. There is much that I must remember to speak for this medal, to tell its story as it should be told. I must remember not only the great secret with which I was trusted, but also all that happened to me and those like me. That is a lot. But I think that I can do it well enough. After all, I was expected to remember, as were the other men trained with me. The lives of many men depended entirely on our memories.

Look here. The man you see riding a horse on the back of this medal was an Indian. He is also one of those raising that flag there behind him. I knew him when we were both young men. His name was Ira Hayes. He was a fine person, even though he was not one of our people, but *Akimel O'odam*, a Pima Indian. We both fought on a distant island far off in the Pacific Ocean. There was smoke all around us from the exploding shells, the snapping sound of Japanese .25 caliber rifles, the thumping of mortars, and the rattling of machine guns. We could hear the pitiful cries of wounded men, our own Marines and the enemy soldiers, too.

It was a terrible battle. But our men were determined as they struggled up that little mountain. On top of it is where Ira was photographed, raising the flag of *Nihimá*. I was not one of those who fought to the top of Mount Suribachi, but I had my own special part to play. I helped send the message about our success, about the brave deeds so many Marines did that day for *Nihimá*.

*Nihimá*, "Our Mother." That is the Navajo word we chose to mean our country, this United States. It was a good name to use. When we Indians fought on those far-off islands, we always kept the thought in our minds that we were defending Our Mother, the sacred land that sustains us.

*Nihimá* is only one of the Navajo words we chose for places with *bilagáanaa* names. South America became *Sha-de-ah-Nihimá*, "Our Mother to the South." Alaska we called *Bee hai*, "With Winter." Because we knew that Britain is an island, we gave it the name of *Tó tah*, "Surrounded by Water." When we did not know much about a place, we described something about the people there. So we named Germany *Béésh bich'ahii*, "Iron Hat," and Japan was *Bináá'ádaálts'ozí*, "Slant-eyed."

Sometimes we didn't know much about either the country or the people there, but that did not stop us. We used our sense of humor and played with the English. The word we used for Spain was *Dibé diniih*, which means "Sheep Pain."

But I am getting ahead of myself. I have not even explained to you yet why we made up such names. I have not told you why being able to speak our Navajo language, the same Navajo language they tried to beat out of me when I was a child, was so important during World War Two. It was because I was a Navajo code talker.

What was a code talker and what did we code talkers do? Why was the secret we shared so great that we could not tell even our families about it until long after the war ended?

You cannot weave a rug before you set up the loom. So I will go back to the beginning, pound the posts in the ground, and build the frame. I will start where my own story of words and warriors begins.

# CHAPTER ONE
## Sent Away

I was only six years old and I was worried. I sat behind our hogan, leaning against its familiar walls and looking up toward the mesa. I hoped I would see an eagle, for that would be a good sign. I also hoped I would not hear anyone call my name, for that would be a sign of something else entirely. But the eagle did not appear. Instead, my mother's voice, not much louder than a whisper, broke the silence.

"Kii Yázhí, come. Your uncle is in the wagon."

The moment I dreaded had arrived. I stood and looked toward the hills. I could run up there and hide. But I did not do so, for I had always obeyed my mother—whose love for me was as certain as the firmness of the sacred earth beneath my moccasins. However, I did drag my feet as I came out from behind our hogan to see what I knew I would see. There stood my tall, beautiful mother. Her thick black hair was tied up into a bun. She was dressed in her finest clothing—a new, silky blue blouse and a blue pleated skirt decorated with bands of gold ribbons. On her feet were soft calf-high moccasins, and she wore all her silver and turquoise jewelry. Her squash-blossom necklace, her bracelets, her concha belt, her earrings—I knew she had adorned herself with all of these things for me. She wanted me to have this image of her to keep in my mind, to be with me when I was far from home.

However, the thing I saw most clearly was what she held in her arms. It was a small bundle of my clothes tied in a blanket. My heart sank. I really was going to be sent away.

My mother motioned toward the door of our hogan and I went inside. My great-grandfather was waiting for me on his bed. He was too weak to walk and was so old that he had shrunk in size. He had never been a big man, but now he was almost as small as me. Great-grandfather took my hand in both of his.

"Be strong, Kii Yázhí," he rasped, his voice as creaky as an old saddle. I stood up on my toes so that I could put my arms around his neck and then pressed my cheek against his leathery face. "Kii Yázhí," he said again, patting my back. "Our dear little boy."

I had always been small for my age. My father used to tease me about it, saying that when I was born he made my cradleboard out of the handle of a wooden spoon. My baby name was Awéé Yázhí. Little Baby. Little I was and little I stayed. I went from being Awéé Yázhí, Little Baby, to Kii Yázhí, Little Boy.

"You are small," my grandfather said, as if he could hear what I was thinking. "But your heart is large. You will do your best."

I nodded.

When I stepped outside, my mother bent down and embraced me much harder than my grandfather had hugged me. Then she stepped back to stand by the door of our hogan.

"Travel safely, my son," Mother said. Her voice was so sad.

My father came up to me and put his broad, calloused hands on my shoulders. He, too, was wearing his best clothing and jewelry. Though he said nothing, I think Father was even sadder than my mother, so sad that words failed him. He was shorter than her, but he was very strong and always stood so straight that he seemed tall as a lodgepole pine to me. His eyes were moist as he lifted me up to the wagon seat and then nodded.

My uncle clucked to the horses and shook the reins. The wagon lurched forward. As I grabbed the wooden backboard to steady myself, I felt a splinter go into my finger from the rough wood, but I ignored the pain. Instead I pulled myself around to turn backward and wave to my parents. I kept waving even after we went around the sagebrush-covered hill and I could no longer see them waving back at me, my father with his back straight and his hand held high, my mother with one hand pressed to her lips while the other floated as gracefully as a butterfly. I did not know it, but it would be quite some time before I saw my home again.

The wheels of the wagon rattled over the ruts in the road. I waved and waved and kept waving. Finally my uncle gently touched me on the wrist. My uncle was the only one in our family who had ever been to the white man's school. His words had helped convince his sister, my mother, to send me to that faraway place. Now he was taking me there, to Gallup, where the mission school was located.

"Kii Yázhí," he said, "look ahead."

I turned to look up at my uncle's kind face. His features were sharp, as hard and craggy as the rocks, but his eyes were friendly and the little mustache he wore softened his mouth. I was frightened by the thought of being away from home for the first time in my life, but I was also trying to find courage. My uncle seemed to know that.

"Little Boy," he said, "Sister's first son, listen to me. You are not going to school for yourself. You are doing this for your family. To learn the ways of the *bilagáanaa*, the white people, is a good thing. Our Navajo language is sacred and beautiful. Yet all the laws of the United States, those laws that we now have to live by, they are in English."

I nodded, trying to understand. It was not easy. Back then, school was such a new thing for our people. My parents and their parents before them had not gone to school to be taught by strangers. They had learned all they knew from their own relatives and from wise elders who knew many things, people who lived with us. People just like us.

My uncle sat quietly for a time, stroking his mustache with the little finger of his right hand. The wagon rattled along, the horses' hooves clopped against the stones in the road. I waited, knowing that my uncle had not yet finished talking. When he stroked his mustache like that, it meant he was thinking and choosing his words with care. It was important not to rush when there was something worthwhile to say.

Then he sighed. "Ah," he said, "your great-grandfather

was your age when the Americans, led by Red Shirt, Kit Carson, made their final war against the Navajos. They wished either to kill us all or remove every Indian from this land. They did this because they did not know us. They did not really understand about the Mexicans."

My uncle turned toward me to see if I understood his words. I politely looked down at my feet and nodded. I knew about the Mexicans. For many years, the Mexicans raided our camps and stole away our people. We were sold as slaves. So our warriors fought back. They raided the villages where our people were held as slaves, rescuing them and taking away livestock from those who attacked us.

"When the Americans came," my uncle continued, "our people tried to be friends with them. But they did not listen to us. They listened to the Mexicans, who could speak their language and said that we were bad people. Instead of helping to free us from slavery, the Americans ordered all the Navajos to stop raiding the slave traders. Some of our bands signed papers and kept the promise not to raid. But each Navajo band had its own headmen. Not all of them signed such papers. So, when all of our people did not stop raiding, the Americans made war on all of the Navajos. They burned our crops, killed our livestock, and cut down our peach trees. They drove our people into exile. They sent us on the Long Walk."

Again my uncle paused to stroke his mustache and again I nodded. I had heard stories about the Long Walk from my great-grandfather. The whole Navajo tribe was forced to walk hundreds of miles to a strange and faraway place the white men called Fort Sumner. Hundreds of our people died along the way and even more died there. The earth was salty and dry. Our corn crops failed year after year. Sometimes late winter storms swept in and men froze while they were trying to work the fields. Our people began to call that place *Hwééldi*, the place where only the wind could live. Our people had no houses, but lived in pits dug into the earth. Indians from other tribes attacked us. We were kept there as prisoners for four winters. Even though I was a little boy, I knew this history as well as my own name.

"Kii Yázhí," my uncle said, his voice slow and serious as he spoke. "It was hard for our people to be so far away from home, but they did not give up. Our people never forgot our homeland between the four sacred mountains. Our people prayed. They did a special ceremony. Then the minds of the white men changed. Our people agreed never again to fight against the United States and they were allowed to go back home. But even though the white men allowed us to come home, we now had to live under their laws. We had to learn their ways. That is why some of us must go to their schools. We must be able to speak to them, tell them who we really are, reassure them that we will always be friends of the United States. That is why you must go to school: not for yourself, but for your family, for our people, for our sacred land."

As my uncle spoke, I saw my great-grandfather's face in my mind. There had been tears of love and pity in his eyes as I left our hogan. I knew now that he had been remembering what it was like when he had been forced to go far away from home. He had been praying life would not be as hard for me at school as it had been for him at Hwééldi.

My uncle dropped his hand onto my shoulder. "Can you do this?" he asked me.

"Yes, Uncle," I said. "I will try hard to learn for our people and our land."

We had reached the hill that marked the edge of our grazing lands. I had never gone beyond that hill before. As my uncle clucked again to the horses, I noticed the pain in my finger and saw the splinter still lodged in it. I carefully worked it free. The tip of that thin needle of wood was red with my blood. Before we went over the hill, I dropped it onto the brown earth. Although I had to go away, I could still leave a little of myself behind.

# CHAPTER TWO
# Boarding School

The boarding school was more than a hundred miles from my home, so our journey took us several days. We slept out under the silver moon and the bright stars. Each morning my uncle cooked food for us over the fire, usually mutton and beans. Those meals were so good and the time I spent with him was precious to me. I knew I was soon going to be away from all of my family. I shall never forget that journey.

However, what I remember most is the morning of my arrival at Rehoboth Mission. It did not begin well for me. As soon as my uncle reached the gate of the school, like all the other parents and relatives who had traveled far to bring their children there, he was told that he had to go. He patted me one final time on my shoulder, stroked his mustache with his other hand, and nodded slowly.

"You will remember," he said.

He watched me walk through the gate before he climbed back up onto the seat of the wagon, lifted his reins, clucked to the horses, and drove off without looking back. He did not say good-bye. There is no word for good-bye in Navajo.

So I was left standing there, a sad little boy holding tight against my chest the thin blanket in which my few belongings were tied. But I was not alone. There were many other

Navajo children standing there, just as uncertain as I was. Like me, those boys and girls were wearing their finest clothing. Their long black hair glistened from being brushed again and again by loving relatives. The newest deerskin moccasins they owned were on their feet. Like me, many of them wore family jewelry made of silver, inset with turquoise and agate and jet. Our necklaces and bracelets, belts and hair ornaments, were a sign of how much our families loved us, a way of reminding those who would now be caring for us how precious we were in the eyes of our relatives.

Suddenly, as if everyone had remembered their manners all at once, we began to introduce ourselves to each other as Navajos are always supposed to do. We said hello, spoke our names, told each other our clans and where we were from. As you know, our clan system teaches us how we were born and shows us how to grow. By knowing each other's clan—the clan of the mother that we were born to, the clan of the father that we were born for—we can recognize our relatives.

"*Yááťeeh*," a tall Navajo boy with a red headband said to me. "Hello. I am Many Horses. I am born to Bitter Water Clan and born for Towering House. My birthplace is just west of Chinle below the hills there to the west."

Hearing his polite words made me feel less sad and I answered him slowly and carefully. "*Yááťeeh*. I am Kii Yázhí. I was born for Mud Clan and Born to Towering House. My birth place is over near Grants. I am the son of Gray Mustache."

A round-faced girl wearing a silky shawl stepped closer

to me and bowed her head. "Hello, my relative," she said. "I am Dawn Girl. I, too, was born to Mud Clan. I am born for Corn Clan."

It was not always easy for me to understand what those other boys and girls were saying. Even though we all spoke in Navajo, we had come from many distant parts of Dinetah. In those days, our language was not spoken the same everywhere by every group of Navajos. But, despite the fact that some of those other children spoke our sacred language differently, what we were doing made me feel happier and more peaceful. We were doing things as our elders had taught us. We were putting ourselves in balance.

Suddenly a huge white man with a red face appeared on the porch above us.

"Be quiet!" he roared at us in English.

Even though most of us could not understand the words he shouted, we all stopped talking. For a moment, before we remembered it is impolite to stare, we all looked up at him. Many of us had seen white people before, when we went to the trading posts with our elders. Almost every trading post was run by white men. Most of them also had their wives and families with them. Because there were no other kids around, those *bilagáanaa* boys and girls often played with the Navajo children. Some of those white traders' children even learned to speak Navajo pretty well—at least much better than their parents.

It is not easy for other people, even other Indians, to learn to speak Navajo properly. The traders always tried to use a little Navajo, but they knew very few words. Sometimes they thought they were saying one thing when they were saying something quite different. I liked to hear the funny way the trader at our post tried to talk Navajo. But I kept a straight face because it would have been rude to laugh at a grown-up, even a grown-up *bilagáanaa* who had just said that all sheep above the age of six should be in school.

However, even though most of us had seen white men before, none of us had ever seen one like that red-faced white man who yelled at us on my first day at the boarding school. His skin was so red that it seemed to be burning. His hair was also that same fiery color. Moreover, his hair was not just on top of his head—where thick hair is supposed to be. It was all over his face. Among Navajos, some men may allow a little hair to grow on their upper lip—just as my uncle and my father did. But this red man had as much hair on his face as an animal. It was on his cheeks, his chin, his neck. Thick red hair even grew out of his ears. He pointed his finger and yelped more words that none of us understood.

"Is that a man speaking or is it a dog?" one of the boys next to me whispered in Navajo.

He wasn't joking. It was a serious question. The huge white man's angry shouts did sound like the barking of a dog. We all put our heads down as that red-dog white man yelped and roared. Finally, he became silent. But he kept staring down at us, waiting for something. When none of us moved, but just stood there, politely looking down at the ground, he barked at us again even louder.

We did not realize that he was ordering us to lift up our faces. We could not understand that he was telling us we must look at him to pay attention. None of us yet had learned that white people expect you to look into their eyes—the way you stare at an enemy when you are about to attack. Among *bilagáanaas,* the only time children look down is when they are ashamed of something.

"What does he want?" a girl whispered in a frightened voice. "He seems angry enough to eat us."

A dark-skinned man with a kind face walked up to stand beside the big, red white man. The red white man growled something at him and the dark-skinned man nodded. Then he turned to us.

"*Yáát'eeh,* my dear children," he said in Navajo in a comforting voice. "My name is Mr. John Benally. I am born to Salt Clan and born for Arrow Clan."

That was when all of us realized this dark-skinned man was Navajo. We had not even thought he was any kind of Indian at all before he spoke. It was not just because he was dressed like a white man, but because his hair was so short. He wore no hat and you could see that all his hair had been cut off close to his scalp. We had never seen a Navajo man with such short hair. Back then, all Navajo men were supposed to have long hair.

Realizing that this man, dressed like a white man, was a Navajo made us look around the school yard. We had already noticed there were many older boys and girls there, all in uniforms. We had thought they were *bilagáanaa* children. They were watching us silently. Now we looked at them differently, seeing that their emotionless faces looked Navajo. But none of them had come to introduce themselves.

Many Horses, the tall boy with the red headband, spoke up.

"My uncle," he said to Mr. John Benally, using the polite form of address to show he respected this man like a relative, "are those other children in *bilagáanaa* clothing also Navajos?"

"Yes, my nephew," Mr. John Benally said, "but I am sorry that I must now tell you something. Listen well. You are forbidden to speak Navajo. You must all speak in English or say nothing at all."

All of us stood there in silence. Most of us did not know any words in English. Those who did know some English words were so shocked that they could not remember any of them. Finally, Mr. John Benally helped us.

"Children," he said in Navajo, "here is a word of greeting that you can say. Watch how I hold my mouth and then repeat it after me. Heh-low. Heh-low."

All of us did as he said. We opened our mouths and made those two sounds. "Heh-low, heh-low, heh-low."

We hoped that this kind Navajo man would stay with us and keep talking Navajo. His job as an interpreter, though, was for one day and one day only. After that he went back to working in the stables and speaking broken English.

The only way left to us was to speak English. Thinking back on it, years later, I see now that it was a good policy in one sense. In the weeks that followed, we learned

English much more quickly because we could not use our native tongue. But I can never forget how sad it made me feel when I learned enough English to understand what the angry, red white man, whose name was Principal O'Sullivan, had to say about our sacred language and our whole Navajo culture.

"Navajo is no good, of no use at all!" Principal O'Sullivan shouted at us every day. "Only English will help you get ahead in this world!"

Although the teachers at the school spoke in quieter tones than our principal, they all said the same. It was no good to speak Navajo or be Navajo. Everything about us that was Indian had to be forgotten.

# CHAPTER THREE
## To Be Forgotten

They took away our hair.

"My children," Mr. John Benally said, after teaching us how to say hello in English, "I am sorry, but you must go now into this room."

We did as he asked. One by one we were herded into a little shed where three tall, uniformed Navajo boys, whose hair was as short as Mr. John Benally's, were waiting.

I should explain, grandchildren, that in those days, among our people, both men and women always kept their hair long. It was a sacred thing. Cutting your hair was believed to bring misfortune to you. But at mission school they had other beliefs.

I was the first one in line. Two of the uniformed boys took me by my arms, one on each side, and pulled me over to a chair.

"What are you doing?" I said in Navajo, just loud enough so that they could hear. But they did not answer me.

Instead, they pushed me down into that hard wooden chair and held me firmly—as if I were a sheep about to be sheared. Then another boy with a big pair of scissors chopped off my hair. He did it so quickly that it was over almost before I knew it. Another stunned child was being led in, and shoved into that chair even before I was out the door.

Both boys and girls had their hair cut. The only difference was that the hair of the girls was left a little longer than the boys. But I could see from the looks on their faces that losing most of their beautiful hair made those girls feel the same way I felt. Naked and ashamed.

Not only our hair was stripped away. After being shorn, we were led into two separate buildings, one for the boys and another for the girls. Once we were inside, we were made to take off all our fine clothing and our jewelry. We never saw those clothes or jewels again. Years later I learned that our squash-blossom necklaces and turquoise bracelets, earrings and hair ornaments and silver belts, were sold to white men and women.

In exchange for my clothing and jewelry, I was issued a military-style uniform made of cloth that was rough and itchy, and a stiff cap that was shoved down onto my head. The uniform and cap were too big for me, so big that my cap came down over my eyes. That made no difference to the older students who were handing out our new clothing. Once I was dressed I was pushed out onto the school yard. There, we new students were formed into a line and made to stand at attention, with the boys on one side of the yard and the girls, who were now wearing long brown dresses, aprons, and head coverings, on the other.

It was so strange. Where only a few moments before, there had been a colorful crowd of Navajo children, each one different from the other, now we all looked just the same. In our drab uniforms, the only difference between us boys was our size. Of course, I was the smallest one. I remember thinking that they had removed from us every-thing that we owned. But I was wrong. There was still one more thing to be taken.

We were led one by one to stand in front of a skinny white man with yellow hair who was sitting at a desk. A white board with curved black marks on it was propped up on that desk. None of us could read English, but I learned later that those curving marks that twisted like worms were the letters of the man's name: Mr. Reamer. I also learned later that he always did the job he was about to do with us new students because he had convinced himself that he understood our language.

Mr. John Benally stood close to help with translating as Mr. Reamer asked each child the name of his or her father. That translation would help decide each student's new last name in English. For example, one of the boys in our group said he was the son of *Bilíí daalbáhí,* "One who Has Roan Horses." He became John Roanhorse. Mr. Reamer seemed very fond of the name John and gave it to lots of boys. Also, if he did not like the way someone's last name sounded in English when it was translated from Navajo, he would just choose another last name and give it to that boy or girl.

We did not know it at the time, but some of the last names we got were the names of famous dead white men. Washington, Lincoln, Jefferson, and so on. That was shocking to me when I discovered it later. Among our people no one is ever deliberately given the name of someone who has died.

When it came to be my turn I stood at attention in

front of the desk. The skinny, yellow-haired white man said something to me. What he said sounded very strange. It did not sound like any language I had ever heard before, not even the English that everyone around us was now speaking. Once again the white man made those unpleasant noises. He sounded like someone trying to speak when his mouth is full of food.

"He thinks he is talking Navajo," Mr. John Benally whispered into my ear. "He is trying to ask you the name of your father."

*"Dágháatbáhi Biye',"* I said. "I am the son of the One with a Gray Mustache."

"Huh," said Mr. Reamer as he wrote something down on his paper. "Another Begay."

Because that white teacher could not really understand our language, he did not realize that *Biye'* in Navajo just means "son of." So he made *Biye'* my last name, although he wrote as he heard it—Begay. Lots of other white men at other schools did the same. That is why we now have so many Navajo families like our own with the last name of Begay.

But at least I was not named John. By the time the skinny white man got to me he had already made more than twenty boys John and he was tired of writing that name. So I was given the same first name as that teacher's dead uncle. Ned.

Thus it was, grandchildren, that I began my day as Kii Yázhí and ended it as Ned Begay.

# CHAPTER FOUR
## Progress

TRADITION
IS THE ENEMY
OF PROGRESS

That was written in large letters on the big wooden sign in front of the mission school. It was the first thing we were taught to read. Anything that belonged to the Navajo way was bad, and our Navajo language was the worst.

Without thinking, when I saw Mr. Reamer the second day I was at mission school, I spoke the polite Navajo greeting my parents had told me I should always use to an elder. Instead of greeting me back, he yelled something, slapped his hand over my mouth, and picked me up under his arm like I was a little puppy who had done something bad. He carried me inside to the sink where there was a bar of brown soap floating in a bucket, forced me to open my mouth, and then shoved that big, wet bar of soap into it. He rubbed it back and forth between my teeth so hard that foam came out of my mouth and my nose. The soap even got into my eyes and I couldn't see. I choked and coughed and thought I was going to die.

Finally, Mr. Reamer decided I'd had enough. He ducked my head into the bucket, dropped me on the floor, and just walked away as if nothing unusual had happened. I staggered outside and fell down to my knees. My vision was blurry and my lips were cut and bleeding. Tommy Nez, who was the first friend I made in school, lifted me to my feet. He and another bigger boy I hadn't yet met whose bunk was close to mine, had to help me get back to the dormitory because I could not walk without falling.

"My relative, you will return to balance again," that bigger boy, whose name I later learned was Jesse Chee, whispered in my ear in Navajo. "The Holy People have not forgotten you."

Somehow Jesse Chee knew I had to hear our language just then, though it was a risk even to whisper it. Those teachers had ears that seemed to hear our thoughts. I knew I had found another friend.

I also knew that I never wanted to experience that awful soap again. So I tried my best to avoid speaking Navajo when any adult could hear. I never had my mouth washed out again, but still, to this day, I cannot see a bar of brown soap without feeling a little sick to my stomach.

That same punishment was given to the other boys and girls who spoke Navajo. Whenever they did so, their mouths would be washed out. It happened to Jesse Chee, to Tommy Nez, to Samuel Manyhorses, and to everyone I knew. I don't think a single child escaped having his or her mouth roughly washed out with soap. Most learned their lesson quickly and watched what they said. However, some of the children were not just forgetful about using our language, they were openly defiant. They refused to give up speaking Navajo.

So they were beaten with heavy sticks. Principal O'Sullivan, who was also the head disciplinarian, punished the most defiant children. He had a favorite stick that hung on the wall behind his desk. Sometimes he would beat the boys and girls so badly that they would not be able to walk the next day. John Roanhorse, who also had a bed in my part of the dormitory, was one of the most stubborn ones. His mouth was washed out so often that it no longer seemed to bother him.

"That *bilagáanaa* soap is not so bad," he said to Jesse and Tommy and me one night in the dormitory. "I am getting to like the taste of it."

Even being beaten did not stop John Roanhorse from speaking Navajo. He was the biggest of the boys and he would stand there, taking a beating without crying. Principal O'Sullivan just about wore himself out hitting him. He even broke one of his favorite sticks over John Roanhorse's back. So it was decided that a simple beating was not enough. John Roanhorse was taken into the cold stone basement and chained in a dark corner. He was kept there for a week with nothing to eat but pieces of stale bread and nothing to drink but water. When they brought him out, his eyes seemed as small as those of a mole and there was a lost look on his face. I think a part of his spirit was left down in that cold, dark place.

I was never openly defiant like John Roanhorse had been. Nor was I like the careless boys and girls who kept speaking Navajo when our teachers—who watched us the way coyotes watch a prairie dog hole—could hear them. I did my best to learn English. As the days turned into weeks, then months and years, I began not just to do well in my classes, but to do better than any other student— especially in such subjects as history and geography. Learning and remembering things of the past and finding out about faraway places was interesting to me. I seemed to be a perfect student.

When my *bilagáanaa* teachers looked at me, they saw a little Navajo boy who did just what he was told, never got in trouble, and studied hard. Whenever I was called on, I would stand right up.

"Yes, teacher," I would say, widening my eyes and nodding my head as I spoke.

Yes, teacher! Those were the two words I spoke more than any others when I was in mission school. They were like magic. Even if I did not understand something, all I had to do was say those words to make my white teachers nod back at me or smile. Sometimes they did not even ask me to answer the question.

"Very good, Neddie," they would say.

However, I was stubborn in ways the teachers could not see. I spoke nothing but Navajo whenever I was alone with other Indian students. In the basement of the school or out back behind the wood shed, I learned Navajo songs and stories. Some students in that school, especially after being beaten enough times for talking Indian, reached the point where it became hard for them to speak Navajo, even when they wanted to. But it was not that way for me. If anything, rather than taking my language away

from me, boarding school made me more determin
never to forget it.

So I held on to my sacred language while learning the words and the ways of the whites. But I had no idea, even in my wildest dreams, that the very language those *bilagáanaa* teachers tried to erase—the way you wipe words from a blackboard—would one day be needed by important white men.

At first, my time in the boarding school did not go quickly. In fact, the days were so long that it sometimes seemed as if each one was a year. Despite the boredom and the loneliness, I kept on working hard. Trying to do well became my way of surviving, just as some of the other students got by simply by going somewhere else inside themselves, showing a blank and stupid face to our *bilagáanaa* teachers whenever they were asked to do anything. Then those teachers would shake their heads and go on to someone else. Most of those teachers expected very little of us and that was just what some of us gave back in return. But that was not my way. I have always loved to learn, even though the learning they offered us was much less than that given to *bilagáanaa* children.

Some of my other classmates survived boarding school by throwing themselves into the sports that we played. The older boys had basketball and baseball and football teams. After we younger boys got to know those sports— which none of us had ever seen before being sent off to school—we, too, became great fans. Some of us wanted nothing more than to become one of those heroic Indian athletes like Jim Thorpe, who wore a sports uniform and did great things on the playing field. Whenever we played a game against other Indian schools, I was always among those cheering loudly for our side. But little I was when I came to school and little I stayed. I grew some, but reluctantly. I'd never be more than a few inches above five feet. I was too small to play sports. I couldn't hope to become one of those athletes who recklessly threw their bodies against each other with as much energy as our warriors in the old days had hurled themselves at our enemies.

Even though my body would not grow tall, somehow I knew that there was no limit to the growth of my mind. I read and studied and wrote, and my teachers noticed. I still didn't speak up much in class—that would have been calling attention to myself or embarassing to the other students who did not do so well in their studies. Instead I just did well on my written work, passing tests with high grades and handing in assignments done in perfect English.

"Neddie, you are almost as bright as a little white child," the teachers would say, meaning to compliment me. "You should speak up more in class."

Some of them would even pat me on my head, as if I were a little pet monkey that had just done well at obeying a command.

"Thank you, teacher," I would answer in a voice just loud enough to be heard.

*Someday,* I said to myself, *I will become a teacher, one who does not just teach, but also shows respect to all his Indian students and expects the best of everyone.*

I worked hard with that goal in mind. Because I took such interest in my studies and in that good goal of becoming a teacher, time no longer crawled by like a snail trying to get to the top of a big stone. The hours and days, the weeks and months and even the years, grew legs and began to run like an antelope.

Almost before I knew it, the day came when I graduated from the mission school. For many Navajo students, this was the end of formal education. But I had done so well that I was accepted into the high school program. It made me so happy. There were two good things about the high school program. The first and best was that instead of being a journey of many days, Navajo High School was only twenty miles away from my home. I would still be living in a school dormitory, but now I would be close enough to visit my parents often and the younger brothers and sister who had been born during my years at boarding school. At the old school, I could only go home summers. Now I would be with my family every weekend and every holiday.

I have said that there were two good things about the high school program. The second was that the teaching was better. Since we had gained that much education, the high school teachers assumed that we were educable. They did not often do such things as use our entire school day cleaning the classrooms and washing the windows of the building. More information was offered to us, along with a real library. I read every book I could get my hands on and welcomed the challenge of better classes. I excelled in English and in social studies.

One social studies paper that I wrote during my first year in high school I remember particularly well. I did not realize it at the time, but it dealt with people and a place that would change my life forever. Those people lived on a group of faraway islands that they called Nippon, but we Americans knew it as Japan. I had read about how those people were having hard times. So I wrote my paper about their suffering. I discussed how difficult it was for them because there were so many of them on their small group of islands. In a space not much larger than our Navajo homelands, there were 80 million Japanese people. They did not have enough wood or coal to heat their homes. Terrible earthquakes had recently shaken their land. Many Japanese had been killed or injured and their homes had been destroyed. They had no food and shelter and were in need of help.

My social studies teacher was a man named Mr. Straight. He was tall and thin with a sharp face as pale as the crescent moon. He wore very small eyeglasses that were always slipping down on his nose. Those glasses fascinated us students. We all expected that one day they would slip right off and fall to the floor. That day, when Mr. Straight nodded his head after I finished reading my paper, those glasses slid down to the very tip.

"Well done, Neddie," he said to me, quickly pushing his glasses back up on his nose and then tapping me on my shoulder with his long bony index finger. "I doubt that your average white student could have said it much better."

Soon after that, we students at Navajo High School had our own food drive for the poor, hungry Japanese.

Even though we came from families much poorer than those average white students, we still were able to collect two big crates of canned goods that became part of the many tons of food relief shipped by America to the islands of Japan.

# CHAPTER SIX
## Sneak Attack

From then on, I took a special interest in Japan. I read everything I could find about it, including articles in newspapers and the few magazines in our school library. To my dismay, things in the island nation began to change in an unexpected way. Their military leaders had decided not to rely on help from the rest of the world. They would go to war to get all those things they needed. They were great warriors, those Japanese, and had been for hundreds of years. In the past, no enemies had ever been able to invade their sacred islands. Now, though, their interest was not in defense. They built up a big army and a navy and attacked other countries around them. Soon they had defeated the Chinese and taken over many other islands in the Pacific Ocean. They said it was their divine destiny. The whole Pacific Ocean was meant to be theirs alone.

On the other side of the world, in Europe, the Germans were saying similar things. It was Germany's destiny to rule their part of the world. They, too, went to war and conquered other nations around them. They formed an alliance with the Japanese.

Many people in America were now worried. They feared that the time might come when America would have to go again over to Europe and fight as they had done in my grandparents' time during World War One. And America had soldiers and sailors in the Pacific Ocean, in the Philippine Islands, and on the islands of Hawaii. They might soon have to defend themselves from the Japanese.

For most Navajos, though, the possibility of a war was very far away. Caring for their herds and trying to make ends meet was all they had time to think about. But our Navajo Tribal Council passed a special resolution in June of 1940. I liked their words so much that I made a copy of them on a piece of paper to carry with me in my wallet. I've kept those strong words all these years, though I have had to recopy them several times when the paper they were printed on grew worn from being folded and unfolded or when it was soaked by the salt water as we landed on those beaches. It is often that way, you know. Strong words outlast the paper they are written upon.

Here is what our tribal council said:

> Whereas, the Navajo Tribal Council and the 50,000 people we represent, cannot fail to recognize the crisis now facing the world in the threat of foreign invasion and destruction of the great liberties and benefits which we enjoy on the reservation, and
>
> Whereas, there exists no purer concentration of Americanism than among the First Americans, and
>
> Whereas it has become common practice to attempt national destruction through sowing

the seeds of treachery among minority groups such as ours, and

Whereas, we hereby serve notice that any un-American movement among our people will be resented and dealt with severely, and

Now, therefore, we resolve that the Navajo Indians stand ready as they did in 1918, to aid and defend our government, and its institutions against all subversion and armed conflict and pledge our loyalty to the system which recognizes minority rights and a way of life that has placed us among the greatest people of our race.

If our help was needed, we Navajos would be ready.

But when the attack finally happened, it seemed that no one was ready. It was December 7, 1941, a Sunday I will never forget.

Bright late autumn sun was shining through the windows of our dormitory, but there was no sun in my heart. In the other corner of the room several of my friends were laughing and talking, but I was in no mood for anything but silence. I was still smarting from what had happened to me two days before. I was so embarrassed. Although, as I have explained, I tried to be careful when I spoke our sacred language, that Friday I had been caught. Mr. Straight overheard me greeting one of my friends in Navajo when I thought no teachers were around. It didn't matter that I could now speak English as well as any *bilagáanaa*. It didn't matter how good my grades had been in all my classes. By speaking one word in our sacred language I had just proved to my teacher that I was as hopeless as the rest of my people.

"Do you want to always be an ignorant, useless savage, Begay?" Mr. Straight had said in a disappointed voice, looking down at me over the top of his glasses. "You must always speak English. Navajo is no good, no good at all."

Then he had placed me in front of the whole class with a dunce cap on my head.

That Sunday, as I sat by the window in the dormitory living room, I had my hand on my head, remembering how that dunce cap felt and how foolish I must have looked to everyone, even though my classmates had all politely averted their eyes from me while I was up there. I was both sad and angry. Would the *bilagáanaas* never respect me because I was a Navajo? Did I really have to give up everything Navajo to succeed in the modern world?

Suddenly Tommy Nez came running into the dormitory living room.

"We've been attacked!" he shouted. "It was on the school radio!"

Some of us looked out the windows to see if the enemies were close by. All that we saw were the familiar hills and the dusting of snow that had fallen the night before. We left the dorm and went running to the main school building where the radio was located. Mr. Straight was at the front door.

"Come with me," Mr. Straight said. His voice was tight and nervous.

He led us all into the hall outside the main office to listen to the radio. It told a terrible story. The Japanese had attacked the United States at a place called Pearl Harbor. Most, if not all, of our planes and boats were destroyed. Many people died.

We turned to our teacher, but he looked as confused as we felt. No one seemed to know what to do or say.

"Perhaps those Japanese will attack the Navajo reservation next," Tommy Nez whispered.

"Be quiet," Mr. Straight snapped, pushing his glasses back up onto his nose so hard that he knocked them off and had to grab them before they hit the ground. "Everyone back to your dorm!"

We did as he said, but nothing was the same anymore. Our whole world had changed. What was going to happen now?

# CHAPTER SEVEN
## Navajos Wanted

Over the next days, we learned more about the air raid on Hawaii. We heard the names of islands thousands of miles away where the Japanese were attacking American and Allied bases in the Pacific. Even I, who loved geography, had never heard about most of those places. I had to look hard through the maps in my geography book to locate them. Wake Island, Guam, Guadalcanal. By Christmas of 1941 all of those places had fallen to the Empire of the Rising Sun.

"You must all sacrifice to help the war effort," our teachers said.

Even though I understood what they meant, I could not help remembering that we Navajos had already sacrificed a lot. Most of our families were still poor because of the government livestock reduction of our sacred herds. None of our people were as wealthy as any of the *bilagáanaas* we saw, especially those who ran the trading posts.

Poor as we were, we Navajos really did want to help. Our tribal council met at Window Rock and declared war on Germany, Japan, and Italy. Navajo men took their guns, packed supplies, and rode their horses in to report to the Indian agent. They did not know how far away Pearl Harbor was, but they were ready to go there and fight the enemy. However, almost all of those men were told they could not be warriors for the United States because they only spoke Navajo or because what English they spoke was not good enough. That made them sad and ashamed.

I wanted to join up, too, and go fight the enemy. I could speak English well, but I was only fourteen when that attack came on Pearl Harbor. That was far too young and I was too small to convince anyone that I was older.

"This war will be over," I said to my friends, "before I am old enough to enlist."

At first, that is what many people thought.

"Now that America has declared war," Mr. Straight said, shaking his bony finger at the sky, "the fighting will soon be over."

Everyone on the radio and in the newspapers agreed. The Axis powers—that was what they called Japan, Germany, and Italy—would quickly crumble. Sadly, we were all wrong. As the months wore on, it became clear that this war was going to be a long one.

It also seemed that the U.S. Armed Forces was yet another place where Indians were not wanted. Only a few Navajos had been accepted as U.S. soldiers, all of them men who had been to mission school. There seemed little interest on the part of the U.S. Armed Services in enlisting the help of those of us who had loved this country long before the ancestors of the *bilagáanaas* came here.

Then, in April of 1942, everything changed. A message from Chee Dodge, our Navajo tribal chairman, was sent around the reservation by shortwave radio. A Marine recruiter was coming to Fort Defiance looking for Indian volunteers. Not just any Indians, but Navajos. Navajos were needed for special work. The federal Bureau of Indian Affairs had given its sanction for Navajos to join up. However, only men fluent in both English and Navajo were wanted.

When I heard that announcement on the radio, I could hardly speak.

"Navajos!" I finally managed to say to my friends. "Navajos! They want Navajos! Did you hear that?"

I was so excited and talking so fast that they teased me.

"Are you sure that's what they said?" Tommy Nez asked me.

"*Wehee*," Jesse Chee said. "Yeah. Didn't they say they wanted Mexicans?"

But that radio announcement interested those guys, too. Our high school was not far from the tribal offices in Fort Defiance. The Marine Corps recruiter was scheduled to speak the next morning, a Saturday, which meant we had no classes to attend. So the three of us went down there together, just to look at that recruiter. He had been given an office right near our Navajo tribal headquarters and we could see that the door was open.

We quietly crept up and peeked through the door. A tall, broad-shouldered white man wearing a neat, well-pressed uniform sat at a desk. He seemed very serious. He sat with his back straight, writing something on a pad of paper. Perhaps it was the recruiting speech that he was about to give.

We were perfectly quiet. I am sure he did not notice us peering in. He was impressive to see, but what was even more impressive were the things hung on the walls around him.

"Look at that," Jesse Chee whispered, pointing with his chin.

We looked. There hung a beautiful sword in a silver case. Just below it was a fine rifle. To either side of the rifle and sword were posters that showed Marines standing tall in their full dress uniform. One of them, in the most colorful poster of all, looked much like the recruiting sergeant himself. However, the uniform of that poster Marine was much more striking than his.

That uniform! Ah! It was so beautiful to behold. The coat and trousers were made of cloth that was as shining and blue as the sky. The cap and gloves were white as clean new snow. The leather boots were as black and polished as jet.

"Did you see the uniform in that picture?" Tommy Nez said after we were back out in the street. "Boy, that was sharp! I'd sign up just to have a uniform like that one!"

The three of us decided to hang around until that straight-backed white Marine gave his talk at 11:00 A.M. It was quite a speech.

"My name is First Sergeant Frank Shinn," he said in a loud, clear voice as he stood on the steps of the tribal offices, looking out at the crowd of people who had gathered around.

Looking back on that day, I wonder what he thought of those Navajos gathered there in front of him. Some in the crowd, like my friends and me, were short-haired and dressed much like any white man would dress. Only the brown of our faces gave away the fact that we were something other than the usual people who would hear such a recruiting speech. But there were also many in that small crowd who were far different from those he was probably used to seeing. There were men with blankets over their shoulders and rifles in their arms, men wearing headbands or tall black hats, women in long colorful dresses with shawls. The glitter of silver and the glow of turquoise shone out from that crowd in the shape of necklaces and bracelets and earrings on the women, belt buckles and hat bands on the men. No one stared up at the first sergeant, yet there was complete silence as he spoke.

"I'm a Marine and proud to be one," First Sergeant Shinn continued, his voice echoing down the street. He looked around the crowd, as if daring anyone to contradict him. "The Marines need a few good men. There will be real opportunity for you if you enlist. It will be better for you than staying here on the reservation. As a Marine, one of the proud and few, you will have the chance to travel, learn new skills, and meet interesting people."

Of course, he did not mention that some of the interesting people you would meet might be holding guns and sharp samurai swords, shouting *Banzai!* and trying to kill you. If he had, I still do not think it would have frightened away any Navajo recruits, even though some who enlisted that day and in the days following figured that they were heading for some kind of desk job and not into combat.

It seemed to me that this Marine recruiter was telling

us the truth. We Navajos have listened to white men speak for a long time and we have learned to tell when one is trying to deceive us. You can tell a lot about a man by the way he speaks and the way he carries himself. Looking at First Sergeant Shinn, I could see that this was indeed a man who believed in what he said. I was ready to believe it, too. I wanted to become one of the proud and the few.

But there was a problem. They were only accepting men between the ages of seventeen and thirty-two. I was still only fifteen years old.

Yes, grandchildren, this was quite a problem. But right away I thought I saw a solution. In those days, none of us had birth certificates. Nearly all of us were born at home and not in hospitals, with only our families and a midwife present. As a result, the only way the *bilagáanaas* knew the age of any Navajo was based on what age that person or the person's family said. If my parents claimed I was old enough, I could enlist. I went home and told my parents what I wanted them to do. They listened carefully.

"Son," my mother said, "wait outside while your father and I talk of this."

I did as they asked. As I sat leaning against the wall of our hogan with the warm sun on my face, I could hear their soft voices speaking, but I could not understand what they were saying. A lizard ran up to my feet, stopped, bobbed up and down, and then ran off again. Finally my parents called me back in.

"Son," my father said, "we are proud of you. What you

want to do is a good thing. However, your mother and I both think that you are not yet old enough. You are still too young to become a Marine. Wait through another winter. If this war is still going on, then we will give you our blessing to join up."

I was disappointed, but I did as they asked and went back to school. So it was that I was not part of the first Navajo platoon, those twenty-nine men who developed our secret code.

# CHAPTER EIGHT
## New Recruits

Meanwhile, the interviews to find that first group of Navajos for "special duty" were going on. Two weeks passed before they had finally chosen all of the men they wanted for that first group, twenty-nine in all. Each man was physically examined at Fort Defiance Public Health Service and carefully questioned to be sure he was really able to speak both Navajo and English fluently. Each man's age was checked, too. No one over thirty-two or under seventeen was supposed to be accepted. But one of those chosen, Carl Gorman, was actually thirty-five— although he listed his age as thirty-two. Another man, William Yazzie, was only sixteen, but said he was a year older.

All through this period of selection, no one was told what the special duty would be. Early on the morning of May 4, 1942, those twenty-nine men of what would be the first all-Navajo platoon, the 382nd, boarded a bus at Fort Defiance. Some of their friends and families watched as that bus headed southeast in the direction of Tsoodzit, Mount Taylor, the sacred peak that marks the southern boundary of Dinetah. Then they were gone, vanished. It was as if they had fallen off the face of the earth, for no word was heard from them. Not a single letter was received by any of their families who had been left behind. A month passed and then another month.

Now their families back home were getting worried. Some knew a little bit about the armed forces from having served in World War One. After six weeks of boot camp, new recruits are always given a ten-day pass. But not one of those twenty-nine men came home on leave and there were still no letters. Wilsie Bitsie's father was a schoolteacher. His son had promised to keep him informed of how he was doing. Carl Gorman's father was influential in the politics of our tribe and a successful businessman. Both Mr. Bitsie and Mr. Gorman decided to do something. They wrote directly to the Marines and complained to the Indian agent. They expected answers, but when those answers came, they were not very satisfactory. All they were told was that their sons were doing well. But they were on special duty and could not communicate with anyone.

After a while, when no one had heard anything from those first twenty-nine Navajos, people began making jokes about what must have happened to them. One joke was that the white men must have eaten them. When someone said that to me, knowing how much I still wanted to be a Marine myself, I had an answer for them.

"Well," I said, "I have always wanted to see what it was like in a *bilagáanaa* kitchen."

Those jokes finally stopped four months later when one of those twenty-nine men suddenly reappeared at Fort Defiance. When he had left, we had simply known him as Johnny Manuelito. He had graduated from Navajo

High School several years before and was still remembered there as a serious and hardworking student. Now he was a different man. He was Corporal Johnny Manuelito of the 382nd and he wore the bright, impressive uniform of a U.S. Marine. The other Navajo men of the first twenty-nine had been sent on assignment overseas, but he and John Benally, another member of the Navajo 382nd, had been given a different job. They were staying on as instructors for the next group of Navajo recruits.

Johnny Manuelito's duty was to recruit from our eastern half of the big Navajo reservation. He did so in style, wearing his spotless new corporal's uniform as he spoke on street corners and in chapter houses. People were impressed, not just by his words but by how he looked. Those who had known him before said that he truly seemed to be a different person. He looked to have grown taller during the short time he was gone and he carried himself more like a white man than an Indian. When he came to our high school and spoke to the student body, his words reverberated in my mind like drumbeats.

"The Marines," he said, "are the best of the best. We are always the first to fight. Our motto is *Semper Fidelis*, always faithful." He looked like an eagle staring down from a high mountain crag as his eyes swept over his audience of awed young Navajo men. "Soon you may be called up to fight by the draft. If that happens, you will not be able to choose which branch of the armed forces to join. If you make your decision now, you can be sure that you will join the proud and few and become a Marine."

I was thrilled by his words and by the way he looked. I had never seen any Navajo who stood up so straight in the presence of important white men like our principal and several businessmen who sat behind him on the stage as he spoke. They were intent on his every word. He carried himself with such self-assurance and pride that even those big *bilagáanaas* were impressed.

When his talk was over, I quietly made my way up to the front to listen to more of what he had to say. I did not ask him any questions, but listened closely as he spoke. He believed that any Navajo joining up would have a better chance of getting through boot camp than your average *bilagáanaa*. His own platoon had been the first ever all-Indian platoon in the history of the Marines and his instructors had not known what to expect. But the Navajos had surprised them all.

"In Boot," Johnny Manuelito said, "a good many of those average men who hope to be Marines can't stand up to the physical challenges." He swung his hand to one side in a dismissive gesture. "They wash out. It's too hard for your average man to get used to marching long distances and carrying heavy packs, to running and climbing obstacles. It is too difficult to be brave in the face of gunfire. In most recruit platoons, there are even men who have never held a gun."

When he said that, some of us turned to look at each other. It was hard to believe that anyone, man or woman, could grow up to adulthood without ever having used a gun. Every one of us carried a rifle when we hunted to provide food for our families or when we were out at sheep camp and had to protect our herds from creatures that might hurt them.

"Do you know how many of the twenty-nine men in our platoon washed out?" Johnny Manuelito asked us. "Not even one!"

I was not surprised. Those things that he said a Marine recruit needed to learn were part of our everyday Navajo life back then. We were used to walking great distances over hard terrain while carrying things. We would stay out with our herds of sheep overnight and in the worst weather. Going for two or three days without eating was not unusual for us, even those of us who had gone off to boarding school.

I did not sign up that day, but my mind was made up. Even though I was now sixteen and even though I was still small for my age, I knew in my heart that it was my time to serve as a warrior. I would wear a beautiful uni-form and go to see strange places. I would wait no longer. Soon, very soon, I would finally become a Marine!

# CHAPTER NINE
## The Blessingway

Once again, I went to my parents.

"I have done as you asked," I told them. "I have waited a year. Now I want to go and be a warrior to fight for our people. I ask your blessings to become a Marine."

My parents were sad, but they saw that I was determined. I had kept my promise. So, even though it was not yet the end of the school year, they gave me their permission. However, there was one thing I had to agree to before I went to enlist. I had to go with my parents to a singer who would do a ceremony for me. With the protection of *Hózhǫ́ǫ́jí*, "the Blessingway," I might be kept safe when I went into danger. I was glad to do that. The Blessingway is done for all that is good. That is its only purpose.

The singer we went to was Big Schoolboy. That was his Navajo name, Olta'i' Tsoh. He was also known as Frank Mitchell, although I always addressed him as Hosteen, our Navajo word that is a term of respect. He and my uncle were good friends, having gone to school together at Fort Defiance. My uncle had worked with him over the years when Big Schoolboy ran a freighting business, carrying goods back and forth by horse-drawn wagon between his home in Chinle and Gallup. Big Schoolboy also belonged to the Catholic Church, as did most of the members of our family now, especially those of us who had been to mission schools. By the time I reached high school, I was no longer the only one of my family who had been sent off to school. My three younger brothers, my baby sister, and quite a number of my cousins had followed my lead. Although my parents knew less about Catholicism than their children did, they had been baptized and went with us when we attended church. But being Catholic did not mean we would forget the Holy People and our Navajo Way.

It was an honor to have Hosteen Mitchell do the protection ceremony for me. He was a widely respected man—not just a singer, but also a former member of our tribal council. I was also glad because I liked him very much. Respected and important as he was, he was a very modest person, and wise. Best of all, he was fun to be with.

Whenever we were together, he made me laugh. I saw him often when I was home for the summer because I would sometimes help him out with his work. Although he no longer ran a freighting business full-time, he still moved some goods and welcomed my assistance. Even though I was still quite small, by the time I turned sixteen I had grown very strong. I could easily lift bags that weighed more than I did. Because of that, he sometimes called me Wóláchíí', which means "ant." I took that as a joking compliment, as everyone knows that ants are powerful, despite their tiny size.

Since we had both been to mission school, he would tell me stories about his own school days. One of my favorites was about something said by the old priest, Father Duffey. I was riding beside Hosteen Mitchell on his wagon one day when he turned to me and held one finger up to his lips. I knew what that meant. He was about to tell another of his stories about school.

"You know," Hosteen Mitchell said, "it is hard for anyone to speak our language unless he has known it since birth. However, some of the priests thought they could speak Navajo and would try to include it in their sermons. As a result they sometimes said things that were hilarious without meaning to. I am sure you know what I mean."

I nodded, but did not say anything. I did not want to break into his story with my own memories about some of the mistakes I'd heard white men make while trying to talk Indian. I waited politely. A story is better if you have to wait a little bit for it to be spun out.

Hosteen Mitchell gently flicked the reins to encourage the horses as they pulled us up the hill. When we reached the top, he continued his tale.

"There was this one old priest. Father Duffey. He tried to use our Navajo word for people: *Bila' Ashdla'ii*, 'the ones who have five fingers.' He meant to say that all human beings are alike. But instead of saying that all people have five fingers, he said that we all had five of something else." Hosteen Mitchell chuckled. "People tried not to laugh, but every Navajo in the church was just choking as he or she attempted to keep quiet."

Hosteen Mitchell also liked to talk with me about the similarities between our Indian beliefs and those of the Catholics. He did so the day after my parents agreed to allow me to join the Marines. "You know, Wóláchíí'," he said to me, tapping his lip with his long forefinger, "that Golden Rule and those other things that Jesus Christ said people needed to live by?"

I nodded.

"Well," Hosteen Mitchell continued, "that Golden Rule and those other things he did makes me think that maybe Jesus was a Navajo." Then he laughed. "If any of those Christian white traders behaved the way their Bible tells them to live, they would all go broke."

"I think that we do not need to worry too much about that," I said. Then both of us laughed even harder.

I was eager to go and sign up for the Marines, but I knew I would have to be patient and wait for Hosteen Mitchell to tell us when he could do the Blessingway. Perhaps it would be weeks. I wanted to ask him when he would be free to do the ceremony, but since my parents had already requested that he do it, I knew it would be impolite for anyone to ask again. Not a word was said about it when we came back to our hogan that evening. Somehow, I managed to hold my tongue.

Finally, he climbed up onto his wagon to leave. Hosteen Mitchell must have known what was on my mind and had been teasing me by saying nothing. Just before he shook the reins, he lifted his finger up to his mouth as if he had just remembered something.

"Do not forget," he said to my parents, "I will be doing Blessingway next weekend for my big friend Wóláchíí'." Then he winked at me.

Some of you, my grandchildren, have had Blessingway

sung for you. Some of our chantways have been forgotten, but Blessingway is as strong as ever. So you know what it is like to have so many family members and friends and well-wishers gathered around the hogan, all of them putting their minds together to wish success and goodness for you. You know what it is like to be the One-Sung-Over, to be washed in the morning with soapweed, your clothing piled there in front of you on the blanket as the Bathing Songs are sung. You know what it is like to feel the beauty of the sunrise touching you and giving you strength as the corn pollen is sprinkled on the earth into crosses where you kneel. Then you, too, are blessed with that pollen, and you carry the memories of the goodness of Blessingway with you.

So it was for me. I remember looking at the drypainting made by Hosteen Mitchell. Sometimes a Blessingway does not include drypainting. This time, though, nothing was to be left out. I was to be given the utmost help and protection against all the dangers that might come. Hosteen Mitchell's fingers delicately sprinkled golden grains to make the figure of Pollen Boy on the mound where everything was prepared. Then, as the sun reached the middle of the sky, Hosteen Mitchell stood up.

"Bring in the food," he called. "It is the ceremony's day now."

There is not much to say about the time between the noon meal and the evening when the ceremony began again with the blessing of everything from the sacred items and the hogan to all of the personal possessions people had with them. I was free to do what I wanted during that time—with the exception of work. But all I did was find a quiet place and sit, thinking only of the ceremony that was being done for me. I was feeling peaceful and grateful that I was so loved and cared for by my family and our friends. I did not think even once about the journey that would soon begin for me.

Even now, sixty years later, I still feel the beauty of that night. I can hear the twelve Hogan Songs that began the evening, those songs that Talking God sang about the home of Changing Woman, those songs that were sung around the Mountain Where Traveling Was Done. Song after song followed, every one of them chanted by Hosteen Mitchell. These days other singers help out and do some of the songs, but Hosteen Mitchell always did every single song himself. So it went all through the night with songs and blessing. Finally, the Dawn Songs were sung, and then one more song for all those songs that had gone before.

*Haya naiya yana,*
I have come upon it, I have come upon blessing
People, my relatives, I have come upon blessing
People, my relatives, blessed . . .

From there Dawn comes,
She comes upon me with blessing
Before her, from there,
She comes upon me with blessing
Behind her, from there,
She comes upon me with blessing

Behind her, it is blessed,
Before her, it is blessed,
I have come upon it, I have come upon blessing . . .

Hosteen Mitchell took pollen from his pouch and used it to bless my body. He gave me four pinches of pollen to eat and then sprinkled a trail that circled from me to the door and around the south side of the fire. Then he handed me the pollen pouch. I stood and followed the trail outside. I took five steps toward the dawn and stood there, feeling the warmth of the sun touching me. I reached into the pollen bag and took some out to scatter from north to south. I inhaled the dawn four times, giving a prayer to myself, to the new day, and to all that exists.

There was truly blessing all around me and all through me. With that new dawn, with my mind and my body, my spirit and my emotions in good balance, I was ready to begin my journey as a warrior for America.

# CHAPTER TEN
## Boot Camp

The next day was a Monday, but I did not go to school. Instead I went with my parents to the Marine Corps office near our tribal headquarters to sign up. My mother and father waited outside for me while I went in.

First Sergeant Frank Shinn, the very same Marine recruiter I had seen in his office the year before, looked me up and down. I knew he was studying me carefully because I was so small, wondering if I was really old enough. Of course, by then he had seen enough Navajo men to know that it is difficult for white men to tell our age by looking at us.

"Are you at least seventeen years old?" he asked me in a slow voice.

I answered him quickly in English. "I am old enough to join the Marines, sir." I looked back over my shoulder, pointing with my lips out the door. "My parents are waiting outside. They will tell you I am old enough now."

I did not lie to him. I thought that sixteen was plenty old enough. So I was allowed to take the oath and become a Marine. In March of 1943 I joined over sixty other Navajo Indians who took the bus from Fort Defiance to Fort Wingate to be sworn in.

I am sure that some of those men on the bus had the same thoughts that I had as I made that journey. You see, grandchildren, Fort Defiance is the place where our Navajo people were herded together in 1863 to start them on the Long Walk. Their first stop along that hard and painful way was Fort Wingate. Now, eighty years later, Navajos were making that same trip again. This time, though, it was not to go into exile. This time we were going to fight as warriors for the same United States that had treated our ancestors so cruelly.

From what I know now, having talked over the years to many other jarheads—as we Marines call ourselves—my experiences at boot camp were a lot like those of every man who entered the Marines. I was allowed to unpack and relax after we arrived. The other Navajo men and I spent much of that first afternoon and night talking with each other, introducing ourselves, sharing our clans and figuring out how we were related. We were all excited about being there, but also unsure of what would happen next. Some were upset because they had seen the high fences all around us. All those locked gates and guards and barbed wire made them feel as if we had been taken to a prison rather than a training camp. Even though our cots were more comfortable than the beds most of us had been given at Indian boarding school, few of us got any real sleep that night.

The next morning, things began to happen so fast that the world seemed to spin around me. We were taken for another physical and then sent to the barber, where all the hair was cut from our heads. I had been warned by one of the men in our group who had been through reserve officer training that this would happen to me. However, it was still a great shock to watch my black hair falling about my shoulders and down onto the floor, where it was just swept away as if it meant nothing. Even though most of us had already had our hair cut short when we went to Indian boarding school as children, we had never had it all taken off with a razor, as those Marine barbers did. A few quick swipes and there was nothing left up there at all, only skin. Some of the men in our group had tears in their eyes as their hair was shorn. As for me, when I ran my hand over my bare scalp, for some reason all that I could do was shake my head and smile.

"I am a plucked turkey," I said in Navajo to the equally bald recruit who stood up from the chair next to me. We both laughed.

The next step was the supply depot for our standard issue of boots, socks, shirts, and pants.

"These boots," I said, holding them up, "they are too big for me, sir."

"Smallest size made, recruit," said the supply sergeant.

I ended up having to lace them doubly tight. I also learned to stuff the toes with crumpled-up newspaper to keep my feet from sliding around in them.

"And what is this little bag?" I asked.

"Hygiene kit," the bored supply sergeant answered with a hand gesture that told me to move on. "Next."

When I looked inside I saw that it held soap and toothpaste, a toothbrush, and a razor. I looked around at the other Navajo men, some of whom were also looking in their new kits and holding up their razors. Just like me, not one of them had any beard at all. However, despite our lack of facial hair, every Navajo recruit was still expected to put soap on his face each morning and scrape away his imaginary beard. What you did in boot camp did not have to make sense. You just had to do it.

That became even clearer as the day went on. Wherever I went, big men with angry faces yelled at me. No matter what I did, I could not do it right.

"What are y'all ashamed of, recruit?" the drill instructor yelled at me, leaning down so that his nose was almost touching mine. "Y'all lift your head up when I am a-talkin' t' yew, bo-wah!"

I lifted my chin to look up at his face as I had been taught to do in Indian school. However, that did not please him either.

"Are yew eyeballing me, bo-wah?" he bellowed. "Look straight ahead."

"Yes, sir," I replied, turning my head to look away from him while keeping my voice soft to show respect.

"What yew say, bo-wah? Yew speak up now!"

"Yes, sir," I said in a louder voice.

"WHAT?"

"YES, SIR," I screamed. Then he nodded and moved on to his next victim in our line of confused Navajos who had been standing at attention for more than half an hour.

I should add, my grandchildren, that not only did our drill instructor speak English in a strange way, he also used many colorful words and descriptive phrases that I won't repeat. Even among the *bilagáanaas*, those words are not ones most people will say in public. Insulting new recruits, we would learn, was something that drill instructors were required to do. I think it was probably harder for young white men to be abused like that by their drill sergeants than it was for us Navajos. Being Indians, we were used to having white men shout at us and tell us we were worthless and stupid.

As boot camp went on, I actually found that what they expected us to do was pretty simple. There was a routine to every day. All I had to do was listen closely and follow orders.

One purpose of boot camp is to take young men who are out of shape and make them physically fit. However, just as Johnny Manuelito had said, what most young men found challenging was easy for us Indians. A five-mile hike in the sun carrying heavy packs was nothing much for a Navajo used to walking twenty miles to the trading post across a hot dry landscape to carry a hundred-pound bag of flour back home. Running, climbing, and doing calisthenics were easy for me.

It surprised me to see how hard these things were for the white recruits in the other platoons at boot camp. After a long run, they would fall down onto the ground and some would be sick. We Navajos would just stand and wait for the next thing we had to do. No matter what it was, whether it was the obstacle course or crawling under barbed wire while real bullets were fired over us, we Navajos were just about the best.

Even drilling was not a new thing for those of us who had been to boarding school. One of the first things they did at school was to teach all Indian children how to line up and march in step. But I remember one amusing thing about our marching. When you march in the Marines, you count in English like this: "One, two, three, four, one, two, three, four." That is called counting cadence. One day, though, our white sergeant ordered me to count cadence in Navajo. But counting takes longer in Navajo. By the time I had said one—*"T'áá tá'i"*—we had gone three steps.

*"Naaki,"* I counted. "Two." That took two more steps.

"I think," I said in Navajo, "that by the time I reach ten we will all be confused old men."

We burst out laughing. Even the sergeant shook his head in amusement. After that, he stuck to English for marching.

There was also hand-to-hand combat and weapons training. I really enjoyed using those weapons. The first all-Navajo platoon had scored the highest marks ever on the pistol and rifle range. Our second platoon did just about as well. I qualified as an expert marksman. I also liked wrestling. Although I was not tall, I could easily pick up another man much larger than myself and throw him to the ground. But I did not like boxing. Hitting another person with my fists never seemed natural to me.

There was only one thing in basic training that scared most of us. In fact, grandchildren, it almost caused me to wash out. Perhaps I should say "drown out." It was the swimming test. I should have expected it. After all, we were called Marines and were part of amphibious units. That meant we would be called upon to attack the beaches, jumping out of boats and landing craft. I had thought, though, that swimming wouldn't be that necessary. After all, those boats would just bring us right up to shore. I would learn later just how wrong I was about that!

"How many of you sheep herders know how to swim?" our drill instructor growled. "Step forward if you do."

Howard Billiman started to step forward, then hesitated and stood where he was.

The drill instructor shook his head and looked disgusted.

"So what do you weak sisters expect to do if your boat sinks or you have to get across a blankety-blank river once you're out in combat? You think you're going to walk on the blankety-blank water?"

"NO SIR!" we all shouted back.

"No sir, indeed," the drill instructor said, with a sinister smile on his face. "Follow me on the double."

He took us to a big swimming pool and lined us up. One by one, we were blindfolded. Then, without even a word of instruction, we were pushed into the deep end of the pool. Most of us came struggling back up to the surface, coughing and choking and clawing at the water.

"Sink or swim, jarhead!" our drill instructor yelled at us.

Surprisingly, even though we'd never been in deep water before, many of us Navajos did manage to get from one side of the pool to the other. Swimming, it seemed, was something that most people just do naturally when they have to. Those who floundered or panicked were pulled out, had the water pumped out of them, and then were pushed back in again. Real swimming instructions, teaching us how to swim the right way, only began after we succeeded in getting across that pool on our own.

Then it was my turn. Howard Billiman, who had been just ahead of me in line, had actually managed to get from one side of the pool to the other, moving his hands the way a dog paddles with its paws.

I can do that, I thought to myself.

But when they grabbed me all thoughts went out of my head. I was so small that the drill instructor didn't push me in. He lifted me up and tossed me like a rock. And that was how I swam, too, just like a rock. I sank right down to the bottom and did not come up. I stayed there, standing on my feet with my arms held out. I just could not move. Everyone else said they had never seen anything like it. I wasn't struggling, just standing there, holding my breath.

The drill instructor and the swimming instructor had to jump in and fish me out.

"Listen, Begay," they told me, "we're not asking you to live down there in that pool. We want you to get out of it. Understand?"

"Yes, sir," I said.

This time when they threw me in, it was without the blindfold. Just as before, I sank straight to the bottom. But without the blindfold on, it was different. Although things looked blurred and made my eyes feel strange, I could actually see underwater. Step by step I walked across the bottom of the pool until I reached the shallow water and could climb out. I looked over at the swimming instructor. He had his hands over his face. I was not sure if he was laughing or crying.

Eventually, I discovered that if I took a deeper breath I could float up in the water. I did learn to swim, but I was the last man in our platoon to do so.

One funny thing that I learned later, from talking with other non-Indian Marines, was that many white men found it hard to get used to the food served at boot camp.

"Man, that was the worst slop I ever ate," my friend Smitty said to me in the South Pacific while we were sharing our memories of Boot.

I did not know what to say back to him. Like all the other Navajos who went through boot camp, I thought the food was fine. Not only that, there was always enough to eat in the mess hall.

Kee Etsicitty, one of the other Navajo men in our platoon, said just what I felt as we stood in line, filling our plates for the second time.

"*O-lá,* this is sure different from Shiprock Boarding School," Kee said. "Sometimes all we got to eat was one dry tortilla. In our free time, we hunted squirrels and grasshoppers. We even went through the garbage to scrape food from cans and jars."

Most of us Navajos gained weight during the weeks we were in Boot. We'd never seen so much good food before.

It was at boot camp that I began to learn things about white men I'd never known. One day, in the mess hall, a young white recruit came up to me. He was tall, with blond hair and blue eyes. Everybody called him Georgia Boy.

"Chief," Georgia Boy said, "kin y' read?"

"Yes," I told him.

"What's that there say?" He pointed at the sign on the wall.

I wondered why he was testing me like that. Was he one of those people who thought all Indians were too stupid to read? But I read it aloud anyway. "Exit."

"Uh-huh." He nodded. "That's what they tole me it read. So mebbe y' could read me this here letter I just got fum home. The parson helped Ma write it. If you wouldn't mind."

He took a much-folded piece of paper from his wallet and carefully handed it to me.

The letter was not very well written. It mostly said the farm was fine and she surely missed him. There were many X's and O's at the end of it.

"I knows what them is," he said, putting his finger on the X's and O's. "Loves and kisses."

It made me think of the love my own parents had for me. The two of us both sat for a while in silence after I finished reading the letter aloud.

Georgia Boy reached out his hand and I placed the letter in it. He refolded it carefully and put it back into his wallet. Then he took my hand and shook it.

"Thank y'," he said. "Back home in them mountains, I never learnt no reading." He looked over toward our drill instructor, who was walking through the mess hall, and his voice grew low and confidential. "I've managed so far to fool 'em. They all thinks I kin read, but I jes' been putting things to memory. I'm afraid that if they find out they'll jes' kick me right out."

"If you want," I said, "I can teach you."

The smile that came over his face was so broad that I knew I'd made a friend.

All through Indian school we had been taught that white men knew everything. That day, for the first time, I realized several things. The first was that *bilagáanaas* are not born knowing everything. The second was that in many of the most important ways, white men are no different from Navajos. The third? That no matter who they are, people can always learn from each other.

# CHAPTER ELEVEN
## Code School

Finally, graduation day came. Our all-Navajo 297th Platoon finished with the highest honors of all the recruits at boot camp. We held ourselves tall and proud in the uniforms of privates for our graduation photograph.

I did not know what would happen next. In a few days I might be shipped off to the Pacific to fight the Japanese, as other Marines were already doing on the island of Guadalcanal. I'd been reading about their heroic deeds in the *Chevron*, the Marine Corps' camp newspaper. Or I might be trained for some special duty here in the United States. There were only two things of which I was certain. The first was that I was now a real leatherneck. That, grandchildren, is another name for a Marine. It was a good nickname to remind us and everyone else that Marines have always been the toughest of all the armed forces who fight for America. The second thing of which I was certain was that I was now ready for anything.

Many years later, I know I was right about the first thing. We Navajo Marines were tough and determined, perhaps even more so than most of the non-Indian Marines who later served by our sides. Why was this so? It may have been because we remembered the suffering and courage of our grandfathers who fought as warriors to protect our land and our people. We were not just fighting for the United States. We were going into battle for our Navajo people, our families, and our sacred land.

However, as far as that second idea—that we Navajos were ready for anything—we were surely wrong about that. It is true that we Navajos gained a reputation for being especially tough in combat. When a Navajo was wounded in battle, he did not moan or cry out the way many of the other men around us did. He suffered in silence, waiting quietly for help to come to him. This was something we had learned from our elders. They had taught us that in battle you must never give away to the enemy either your weakness or your location. But even though we were prepared for pain, we were not ready for what happened to us next. We were about to enter eight weeks of the strangest training any Marine in World War Two had to go through. In fact, what they asked of us Navajos after we finished boot camp was so unusual and unexpected that many of us thought at first we were the victims of some kind of mean joke.

"297th. Pack your gear. You're shipping out."

That is what the sergeant barked into our barracks the day after our graduation photo was taken.

That was the last thing we had expected. It was Sunday. All of the non-Indian Marines who had been in boot camp with us were leaving on furloughs. They were laughing and joking with each other as they headed for the gate to see friends and family or just go into town and have fun. But not us Navajos.

Some of those lucky guys, like my friend Georgia Boy, waved to us as our bus roared through the gate. I smiled and waved back at him, but my smile was an uncertain one. Why were we sixty-seven Indians being sent out this way, to some destination no one would tell us about? Were we finally going to begin that important but secret task only we Navajos would accomplish? Or was this some kind of punishment?

Our trip wasn't long at all. They took us to Camp Elliott, a little north of San Diego. We were checked into our new barracks without a word of explanation about what we were going to do there. I didn't sleep well at all that night. At 7:00 the next morning, several non-coms, who were to be our escorts, arrived at our barracks. In military language, grandchildren, a "non-com" is a non-commissioned officer, anyone above the rank of a private, but no higher than a sergeant. We were lined up, put through roll call, and then marched off to breakfast. I could hardly eat and a lot of the other guys were just as nervous as I was, picking at their food. As soon as we had finished, we were rounded up again and quick-marched to a building with bars on all the windows and a strong door that our escorts unlocked and opened.

"Inside," the escort sergeant barked.

"Ah, they are taking us to jail," Henry Bahe whispered to me just before we went through the door.

He meant it as a joke, but I didn't laugh. My heart was beating faster. What was happening?

As soon as we all were inside, the escort sergeant shut the barred door and locked it behind him, leaving the rest of the Marines who had escorted us outside on guard. Then he led us down a long hall to another locked door.

It opened to a classroom, much like the ones I had sat in for endless hours at Indian boarding school. The blackboards, the rough wooden floor, the uncomfortable-looking chairs were almost exactly the same. Our escort—who had not set foot into the room—shut the door and once again I heard the sound of a lock clicking.

All that had happened to that point was strange, grandchildren, but it was not as strange as the words I then heard spoken to us from the front of the classroom.

"Be quiet. Be seated."

All of us Navajos turned immediately to look. Those words had been spoken in our native language! There, at the front of the class stood two Navajo men wearing the uniforms of Marines. One of them I recognized at once. It was Johnny Manuelito.

"This is Corporal Johnny Manuelito. I am Corporal John Benally," said the second Navajo man who stood in front of us, speaking in English. "We will be your instructors."

I was stunned. The idea of a Navajo being a teacher was new to me. Yes, grandchildren, I know that many of your teachers are Navajos now. But it was different back then.

Johnny Manuelito and John Benally passed out pencils and blank sheets of paper and then went to the front of the room by the blackboards. I was so amazed by all that was happening that I do not recall being handed a pencil and paper, but somehow I found them in my hands.

"Follow our instructions exactly," Johnny Manuelito said. "We will speak words in Navajo. You must write down those same words on your paper in English." He turned toward John Benally, who held a piece of chalk in one hand and an eraser in the other.

"*Wóláchíí*," Johnny Manuelito said. I looked up in surprise as he said it, then realized he was not looking my way and using my nickname. He was just speaking the word for ant.

In large block letters, John Benally printed the word ANT on the blackboard. As soon as everyone had seen it, he erased it.

"Now it is your turn," Johnny Manuelito said. "We speak in Navajo. You write in English, just as Corporal Benally just did. Be sure to print in block letters." He paused, looked out at all of us, then nodded.

"*Wóláchíí*," he said.

"*Shash*," said John Benally.

"*Mósí*."

"*Bįįh*."

"*Dzeh*."

"*Ma'ii*."

ANT, BEAR, CAT, DEER, ELK, FOX. I put those words down on the paper. But they were speaking so fast that I missed the next few words and could only try to catch up as they continued on.

"*Dibé yázhí*."

"*Na'ats'ǫǫsí*."

"*Neeshch'íí*."

"*Ná' áshjaa'*."

LAMB, MOUSE, NUT, OWL, I printed. By the time they stopped talking I had printed sixteen words. But I still didn't know what this was all about. I glanced around the room. From the looks on the faces of my other platoon mates, they were all confused. Henry Bahe looked as if he was angry. Jimmy King, who was one of the hardest workers of all of us, was shaking his head.

Johnny Manuelito and John Benally went around the room collecting the papers. They looked quickly through the stack and then carefully placed them in a box at the front of the room.

"You have done well," Johnny Manuelito said. "But you must learn to be perfect if you wish to become a code talker."

Code talker. It was the first time I had ever heard that name, but it sounded good to me. Then our two Navajo instructors began to explain our duties to us. The more they said, the better it sounded. Our job was to learn a new top-secret code based on the Navajo language. We would also be trained to be expert in every form of communication used by the Marine Corps, from radios to Morse code. Using our code, we could send battlefield messages that no one but another Navajo code talker could understand.

I realized right away that our job was a really important one. In order to win battles, Marines needed to communicate fast at long distances. In those days before computers, that meant using radio. However, anyone, including the Japanese, could listen to our radio messages. To keep messages secret, the Marines sent them in code. But the Japanese broke every code our American forces used. A new kind of code had to be created.

During World War One, our country had used other Indians, Cherokees and Chickasaws, to send messages in their own language to confuse the enemy. After the war, the Japanese had decided to be prepared for something like that if they had to fight America. They sent people to America to learn not only how to speak English fluently, but also to learn our American Indian languages. Navajo, though, had never been studied. It was one of the hardest of all American Indian languages to learn. Only we Navajos could speak it with complete fluency. Also, because there were so many of us, including hundreds of young Navajo men who had learned to speak English in the boarding schools—our language was chosen for making that unbreakable code.

Where did the idea of using Navajo come from? There was a white man named Philip Johnson who was the son of a white trader on the reservation and so he could speak "Trader Navajo." He liked our people and had Navajo friends. When the Japanese attacked Pearl Harbor, he brought some of his Navajo friends to the Marines in San Diego to demonstrate how our language could be used to send messages.

An important Marine had already been thinking about making an Indian code. His name was Major General Clinton Vogel, commanding general of the amphibious division of the Pacific Task Force. He knew that the U.S. Army was already using Comanches in Europe to send messages in their own language. After hearing of Philip Johnson's demonstration, General Vogel authorized the recruitment of that first class of twenty-nine Navajo

Marines. Just like us, they were brought to Camp Elliott, where they were locked in this same classroom and told to develop an unbreakable code.

Those Navajos did it all by themselves. Some have said that Philip Johnson developed the code and taught it to the Navajos. That is not true. He did not know our sacred language well enough to do this. He was nowhere near Camp Elliott during the summer of 1942 when the code was being created by Navajos. Later on, Philip Johnson came to work at Camp Elliott. His job, with the rank of sergeant, was to be an administrator for the school, help things run well, and write reports. He could not speak the code and never taught it to anyone.

# CHAPTER TWELVE
## Learning the Code

That first day in class, Johnny Manuelito emphasized to us how important our jobs as code talkers would be.

"The lives of many men," he said, "will depend on your messages. You have to get it right the first time. Every time."

Because of its great value, no one was ever to be told about the code. Nothing I wrote down in that room could ever be taken from the room. It all had to be kept stored in only one place: in my head. That was why everything put on the blackboards was quickly erased. Every scrap of paper we wrote on was collected at the end of each day. If I breathed a word about the very existence of the code to an outsider, even to another Navajo Marine who was not a code talker, I could be placed in the brig for the rest of the war.

I have heard it said that we Navajos carried code books with us. That is not so. Some code books were printed up, but they were kept closely guarded. The only two places in the whole world where they were used were our training areas at Pearl Harbor and Camp Elliott. The code went with us everywhere, but only in our memories.

"If you are captured in battle," John Benally said, "die before telling the enemy anything about the code! Even if they beat you, even if bamboo splinters are shoved under your fingernails, you must keep quiet about our secret."

*I will never tell the enemy.* I wrote those words down on my paper and underlined them twice.

John Benally's warning did not frighten me. It made me proud that our sacred language was so important to America. It felt good to know that we were the only ones who could do this useful thing. We swore that we would protect the code with our lives, and we kept our word. I am not sure how many of us became Navajo code talkers during World War Two, but I know that it was close to four hundred men. While it remained classified, not one of us ever told about the code, not even to our families. We kept it secret throughout the war and long after.

How did we make the code work? In fact, grandchildren, it was not hard. First of all, we had to learn a new alphabet. For every letter in the English alphabet, a Navajo word was assigned. *Wóláchíí'*, or Ant, the very nickname that Hosteen Mitchell gave me, was the first alphabet word in our code. That coincidence seemed to me to be a sign that the way of code talking was something I was meant to do and that I would do well at it. *Béésh Doott'izh*, which is "zinc," was the last.

One of our jobs of our second class of Navajo code talkers was to assign more Navajo words to the letters of the English alphabet that are used most often. That is because people who break codes can sometimes do so by hearing or seeing the same sound or symbol appearing many times. They call this "word frequency." So we added seventeen more Navajo words for A, E, I, O, U, D, H, L, N, R, S, and T. The most commonly used of those letters got more than one new word. A became not just *wóláchíí'* for "ant," but also *bilasáanaa* for "apple" and *tsénit* for "axe."

Because it would take far too long to spell out every word that we sent, we only used this alphabet for words that were not used a lot. On Sulphur Island, for example, we spelled out the mountain named Suribachi by sending the Navajo words for Sheep-Uncle-Ram-Ice-Bear-Ant-Cat-Horse-Itch. We used separate code words for things often mentioned in warfare.

There were so many words like that which I had to memorize. Hundreds of them. *Tóó'tsoh*, "whale," was battleship. *Gíní*, "chicken hawk," was dive bomber. *Nímasii*, "potato," was grenade. *So' naaki*, "two star," was major general. Every night I went to bed in our barracks, whispering those words to myself. Each day I was tested in the classroom and taught more words. I did this week after week until the code became as much a part of me as my mouth, my eyes, and my ears. It was not easy, but I was proud to be doing something that only a Navajo could do.

They did try having some young white men learn our code. Major Shannon, another of the Marines who was recruiting Navajos, had been a Bureau of Indian Affairs School principal before he became a Marine. He was convinced that whatever a Navajo could do, a white man could do better. He found three young white men who were the sons of Indian traders. Major Shannon wrote a letter saying they spoke fluent Navajo and insisting they should immediately be made sergeants and given the job of telling the Navajo code talkers what to do. The Marine Corps, however, said those three white men had to go through basic training and start as privates. They would have to prove they were as good as they said. They were not. When it came to things like saying hello, counting from one to ten, or talking about buying coffee and sugar, they did pretty well. But they could not carry on a real conversation. They could not even pronounce many Navajo words right. They were quickly removed from code school and assigned to be ordinary Marines.

Camp Elliott was not all work. Once we began to master the code, we began to have fun. During the last two weeks we were taught such things as how to use and repair our signal equipment. All of our instructors were white Marines who were patient and friendly with us. Because we liked them, we began to play tricks on them and tease them. Even though the Morse code class he taught was so boring that it made us want to go to sleep, Corporal Radant was the teacher we liked best. So we drove him crazy.

What did we do to him? One of the things we did was to practice our weapons drills whenever we had a break in his class. The first rifles we had been issued were old Springfield .03s. Like good Marines, we took them with us to our Morse code classes—with bayonets fixed. Those bayonets were big knives with fourteen-inch-long blades. Whenever the smoking lamp was lit—which meant anyone who wanted to take a break could do so—my friends and I would pick up our rifles and practice bayonet fighting with them. Ah, it was great fun. The fact that we nicked each other now and then and also completely destroyed those old Springfields while we were doing it made it even better. We whooped and hollered and made so much noise as we fenced with our rifles that Corporal Radant finally told us to do our bayonet practice outside. And just to let him know that we were really training hard, every now and then one of us would shove a bayonet through the wall of the tent near wherever he had taken refuge.

Sadly, we had to end our fencing matches when we were issued new M-1 rifles.

The armory sergeant looked down at me sternly as he collected what was left of my Springfield. "Begay," he said, "you get even so much as a scratch on this here new M-1, a big chunk of cash is gonna be docked from your pay."

However, we quickly came up with a new game to keep Corporal Radant's life interesting. Instead of bayonet drill, we started doing hand-to-hand combat during our breaks. Because we had been told by our instructors that a Marine must always be ready to counter an attack, we included our friend Corporal Radant whenever we could. Any time he dared to step outside the tent for a smoke, he found himself wrestled to the ground by a pile of screaming Navajos.

At the end of our time with Corporal Radant he said that he had something he wanted to tell us.

"Because of you," he said in a very serious voice, "I have lost my temper, my health, my good disposition, and my faith in my fellow man, some men in particular."

He looked right at me. I looked back at him, widened my eyes, and then crossed them. Corporal Radant began to laugh. "I am really going to miss you Indians."

Those weeks at Camp Elliott were some of the best in my life. Much hardship and pain and sadness lay ahead of me, but during those weeks—as we prepared for war—I felt at peace. For so many years I had been in schools where I was told never to speak our sacred language. I had to listen to the words of *bilagáanaa* teachers who had no respect at all for our old ways, and who told us that the best thing we could do would be to forget everything that made us Navajos. Now, practically overnight, that had all changed.

Because it was important for us to speak Navajo, we used it with each other much of the time. Unlike at the schools back on the reservation, we were not forced to speak only English. Sometimes, as we chatted with each other in Navajo, the other non-Navajos would look at us, wondering if we were talking about them. But no one ever told us to stop. We were supposed to speak our sacred language here. It felt so good to do this that sometimes it made me want to shout with happiness.

"It is so good," Henry Bahe said to me one day near the end of our training.

I nodded. Those few words of his said it all. It was so good. It was good to have our language respected in this way. It was good to be here in this way. It was good that we could do something no one but another Navajo could do. Knowing our own language and culture could save the lives of Americans we had never met and help defeat enemies who wanted to destroy us.

I think that all of us felt the same way. I could tell by the smiles on their faces, the laughter we shared, and the seriousness with which my fellow code talkers approached our work. Our hearts felt full as we studied the code, took apart and repaired radios in the field, and learned how to fight with our weapons. We were proud to be Marines and even prouder of the role that we had been chosen to play.

Now, grandchildren, when I say we were proud I do not mean that we became self-important. We did not go around thinking we were better than everyone else. We did not boast. Our pride was quiet and humble. We remembered that the language that now could be of such great use, our sacred language, had been passed down to us by our elders. We kept our elders and our families in mind as we studied. We remembered our sacred land.

Each morning, I thought of my home and my family. I stood facing the rising sun. I took corn pollen from the pouch I always carried at my waist, touched it to my tongue and the top of my head, then lifted it up to the four sacred directions as I greeted the dawn. That pouch stayed with me wherever I went during the war. The blessing of that corn pollen helped keep me calm and balanced and safe.

Near the end of our training, we decided to have a special Navajo dance at Camp Elliott to show our appreciation to those who had taught us so much. We also wanted to do something special for our non-Indian buddies, who were going through regular signal corps training and knew nothing about our code. Some of them were very curious about our culture and we figured we could at least share a little of our Navajo way with them.

We got twenty dollars from the camp athletic and morale officer to finance a ceremonial dance. We dressed in blankets and moccasins. We took off our Marine Corps caps and put headbands around our foreheads. Jimmy King, who was one of the best students in our class, played the drum as we danced. We sang the words of the Riding Song and the Bluebird Song as we circled about the camp. It was a good dance and it entertained our white buddies. Some of them clapped their hands and tried to sing along with us. A few even tried to do some dance steps, Corporal Radant and a blond Marine from Boston named John Smith among them. Smitty, as everyone called him, had become one of my own special buddies and I shook his hand when he finished dancing. There was much laughter and many smiling faces that day. Our songs were light-hearted, for we knew that a time lay ahead of us when our hearts might be heavy.

At the end of our program, we had a special surprise. Jimmy King had translated the "Marine Corps Hymn" into Navajo and we all sang it together. Just about everyone knows that song these days, but when we put it into Navajo it came out a little differently.

*"Nin hokeh bi-kheh a-na-ih-la,"* we sang. *"Ta-al-tso-go*

*na-he-seel-kai.*" That meant "We have conquered all our enemies, all over the world."

The last verse was the furthest from the original song. We did not sing it, but chanted it together like a prayer.

"*Hozo-go nay-yeltay to,*" we began. "May we live in peace hereafter." And we ended it this way:

> "*Sila-go-tsoi do chah-lakai*
> *Ya-ansh-go das dez e e*
> *Washindon be Akalh-bi Kosi la*
> *Hozo-g-kay-ha-tehn.*"

It meant "If the Army and the Navy ever see Heaven, the U.S. Marines will be there living in peace."

# CHAPTER THIRTEEN
## Shipping Out to Hawaii

While we were learning to be code talkers, the war had gone on. By the end of August 1943, as our training ended, Admiral Nimitz was getting ready to stage amphibious assaults on the Gilbert Islands with the First and Second Marine divisions. The First and Second had finally managed, after a long and bloody struggle, to secure Guadalcanal in the Solomon Islands. Most people in America, including those in the military, had thought the Canal would be easy for the Marines to take. A few weeks, perhaps a month or two. The Japanese had been tougher than anyone expected. It took no less than six months of furious battle on land, on sea, and in the air. Now those Marines were back on Hawaii, resting and training for their next mission. Among them were the thirteen Navajo code talkers who'd been assigned to the First Division and saw combat on the Gilberts.

Hawaii was where I was going, too. There I'd have further training work with those code talkers who'd experienced battle. I was excited at the thought. Not only was I going to meet other Navajo Marines who'd been under fire, I'd actually be going to one of those faraway exotic tropical islands that had previously only been names on a map for me. Hawaii. People said it was wonderful, like paradise on earth. Just thinking about it made me wonder what other wonderful places I'd get to see. Little did I know how many of those tropical islands would become all too familiar to me in the two years that lay ahead. And most of them would be the opposite of paradise during my stay.

I was assigned to the signal corps of the Third Division. Second Regiment, Third Battalion. We were part of the South Pacific forces commanded by Admiral Halsey. Scuttlebutt around the base was that the Third's job would be to take Bougainville, an enemy air base in the Solomon Islands where the Japanese were dug in deep.

No one ever knows for sure where those rumors come from. But any Marine worth his salt can tell you that it's not a bad idea to listen to the scuttlebutt. It may be closer to the truth than what your commanding officers say. Bougainville. I wondered, could it be as bad as the Canal?

Our two instructors, John Benally and Johnny Manuelito, were shipping out with us. They were excited and happy.

"I did not join the Marines to stand in front of a blackboard," Johnny Manuelito said as a group of us sat around together in the mess hall on our last day at Camp Elliott. He reached into his shirt pocket and pulled out a new piece of chalk. With a big smile on his face, he handed it to Jimmy King. Jimmy and three other men in our second class had been chosen to be the new instructors who'd stay behind and teach the next group of code talkers.

"Now," Johnny said, "it is your turn to try to turn stubborn Navajo sheepherders into signal men!"

Jimmy accepted that piece of chalk with as much seriousness as if it had been a medal. "Thank you, Corporal," he said with a nod. "Next time I see you, I will probably have to call you *T'áá tá'í Béésh tigai,* One Silver Bar."

I shook my head. "No," I said. "Not just a Lieutenant. He will surely be *Naaki Béésh tigai,* Two Silver Bars. Captain Manuelito."

Johnny looked down at his plate and smiled. He was honored and a little embarrassed by the way we had teasingly praised him.

We did not know how wrong we were. As far as I know, not one Navajo code talker was ever raised above the rank of corporal, just as none of us were ever given any kind of official recognition or honor from the time we enlisted until the surrender of Japan. In fact, most of us never even got to wear one of those dress blue uniforms like that first one I saw on the Marine Corps recruitment poster. We were kept invisible. It was partially because our true duty was kept such a secret from so many. But I think it was also because we were Indians in what was still, even in the Marines, a white man's world. It was easy to forget Indians.

I never thought much about promotions at the time, though. There was too much else for me to concern myself with. First there was the journey we were about to take. My initial excitement about the trip had turned to worry. It was a long way from California to Hawaii with a lot of ocean in between. I was going to have to spend many days on a great boat out on the wide waters of the Pacific Ocean. I was not so worried about the Japanese as I was about getting onto that boat and all that water.

Yes, one of my favorite pastimes when I was in Indian school had been to look at the map of the Pacific in my geography book and silently mouth the strange names of those distant islands. Hawaii. Rarotonga. New Zealand. Okinawa. Those daydreams helped me escape from the boredom of boarding school. But I'd never really imagined I'd actually go to such far-off places.

My teachers in Indian school had certainly never encouraged me to think about travel. In fact, they tried hard to discourage such daydreaming. I still remember the day in sixth grade when my teacher, whose name was Mr. Lawson, caught me studying that map of the Pacific when I should have been doing my math. He stood me in the front of the room balancing that heavy geography book on my head.

"Class, do you see this foolish little Indian boy?" Mr. Lawson said, rapping his knuckles so hard on the book that it made my head feel like a bell being rung. "He is wasting his time looking at places on a map that he will never go instead of studying his math. He knows nothing about the world. He will never be smart enough to do anything but herd sheep."

Mr. Lawson was right about one thing. When I joined the Marines I pretty much did not know anything about the world outside of our reservation. Before being sent to San Diego I'd never seen any body of water bigger than a small lake. Of course, I had been taught how to swim. But that was in a swimming pool. A big lake or an ocean was different. Deep water! It scared the pants off me. That Pacific Ocean was huge!

When I was young all Navajos were warned to stay away from deep water. It was always associated with danger. Our old stories tell of water monsters. Things that lived underwater were suspicious to all traditional Navajos. So, even when we got in the Marines, we tried never to eat anything that we knew came from the water. The other Marines thought it was funny at the mess hall on Fridays to watch us Navajos come up to be served.

"Got anything else other than fish?" we'd always say.

A few of us did learn to eat fish, especially on those Pacific islands where there was sometimes little else to eat. But wherever we were, we Navajos were better at finding real meat than any other Marines. After we left an island, there were always fewer chickens and goats and pigs than there'd been when we Indians got there.

The morning before I shipped out, I rose before dawn and prayed with my corn pollen. I asked the Holy People to remember me and help keep me safe on the ocean from the monsters that hid beneath its surface. My fear was not such a foolish thing, grandchildren. Many men got on board those transport ships and never set foot on land again. The Japanese often attacked American convoys with airplanes sent out from their aircraft carriers. Their submarines stalked our ships, sinking them with torpedoes.

Despite my prayers, when the day of embarkation came and they took us down to the pier, I felt as if I was being sent to my doom. Bill Toledo, another of the Navajos in our platoon, saw how nervous I was as we waited for the order to go on board.

"Look up," he said.

I did, raising my eyes to the tall superstructure of the big boat where a U.S. flag was waving.

"No." Bill pointed with pursed lips. "Higher, up there."

I leaned way back to gaze at the blanket of blue sky where a few small clouds hung, white as the fleece of a new lamb.

"Even out on the ocean," Bill said, "Father Sky will be above us. We will never be forgotten by the sky."

At that moment, I felt my fears leave me.

Our voyage to Hawaii was not so hard. The seas were calm and the sunrises beautiful. Father Sky smiled on us. No submarines attacked us and we were kept busy on board practicing our code and all the other skills we needed as signalmen.

I should explain to you, grandchildren, how our teams were set up to use the code. Usually, two Navajos would be out in the field together. One of them would be on the radio, headphones over his ears and the microphone in his hand. He would tune the set to the right frequency. Then he would speak a few identifying words of Navajo into the mike, saying that he was either ready to send or receive in code. As soon as he got the "Roger" from the other end, he would start talking. I was usually the one on the radio set. The second Navajo in the field team would be holding a pad and a pencil. As the radioman got his message in Navajo code, he would speak it out loud to the pencil-and-pad man, who would write it down. After it was written, it could be translated. Then another coded message was sent back.

At the other end, back at the main command post and away from the front line, at least one or two other Navajos would be receiving the messages and doing just what we did. Speaking it, writing it down, translating, and responding. We practiced at working together as smoothly as a well-oiled machine. With all that practice, the trip went faster than I had expected. Almost before we knew it, we reached Hawaii.

I smelled the island before I saw it. The dawn breeze that came from the land was full of the scent of strange flowers and a moist earth that my feet had yet to walk upon. Then I saw Diamond Head for the first time, raising its stone face above Honolulu Bay.

All of the code talkers, both those who had been in the first All-Navajo Platoon and our new group of recruits, were brought together as soon as we left ship at Pearl Harbor. Because we had made changes in the code, we all needed to make sure everyone was well briefed.

Throughout the war, as the code grew, we kept doing that. Code talkers not in combat would be flown in to Pearl or some other convenient location to update everyone on any changes or additions made in the code. It was also a great time for us to catch up on news and learn what had been going on in the war. Because we shared so much information among ourselves and because our code was used for the most important and secret messages, I doubt that any other group of Marines knew more about what was really going on than we Navajos.

When that first afternoon briefing ended I sat outside with Sam Begay and Bill McCabe, one of the code talker teams who'd already seen combat. The wind was coming in from over the ocean and the palm trees were swaying. A little bird with a curved beak was flying around our heads. It was as blue as the sheen of water and it just kept buzzing back and forth among the bloodred flowers of a tall bush that arched over me. It was all so beautiful I could hardly believe it was real.

"What was it like when you got to the Canal?" I asked.

Sam laughed. "None of the officers on our landing craft knew what to do with us Indians. They'd been told we had our own special orders. So we just sort of strolled off the LC onto the beach like two sheepherders looking for a lost lamb."

"We were supposed to report directly to the commanding officer," Bill added, tapping his knuckles on the table. "General Vandegrift. Nobody else. But the landing zone was chaos. We were so green that we didn't wait till we knew things were clear. We just wandered off."

"Happy-go-lucky," Sam said. "Anybody seen a general around here?"

*"Wehee,"* Bill chuckled. "That was us. Dumb as sheep dung. Next thing we knew, we were up near the front line perimeter. We heard this whining sound coming out of the sky like the world's biggest mosquito. Looked up and it was a Japanese Zero."

Sam shook his head. "Diving in low over those coconut palms on a strafing run. Well, we hit the ground, holding on to our helmets while bullets splattered all around us."

"With all the sand we ate," Bill said, smiling, "I figure

each of us was about ten pounds heavier by the time we got up again."

They finally found the general and were sent by him to his signal officer, Lieutenant Hunt, who had also been cleared to know about the secret code. Even though it was late at night, Lieutenant Hunt decided to give the Navajo code a try. With Bill McCabe on one end and Sam Begay on the other, they sent a sample message over the radio. It was received, but not just by Sam Begay.

"Every American radio operator on Guadalcanal heard our message," Bill said. "*Wehee,* did they! They started phoning in to report to headquarters that the Japanese were broadcasting on our frequency. They'd never heard Navajo before and assumed it had to be the enemy. Everybody was so upset and it was such a mess that Lieutenant Hunt called off the test for the night. From then on, every time a message was sent out in Navajo code we had to start it off by saying 'ARIZONA' or 'NEW MEXICO' in a loud voice to alert the other radio operators that we weren't the enemy."

Sam tapped me gently on the arm. "You guys will have to do the same."

"Next day," Bill said, "we picked up where we left off. We still had to prove ourselves. You see, neither the general nor Lieutenant Hunt believed what we were doing would work. No way, no how. Before our code, the only way a coded message could be sent was the white code. You know, that cylinder thing you set a coded message on and then send out by radio . . . tick, tick, tick, like that. Real slow."

"When Lieutenant Hunt gave us the message, I asked him how long it would take with white code," Sam added. "He said at least four hours. I told him we could do it in about two minutes."

"Took us a little longer, though," said Bill. "Seeing as how we wanted to make sure it was a hundred percent right."

"Two minutes and thirty seconds." Sam laughed. "From then on, Lieutenant Hunt was a believer."

# CHAPTER FOURTEEN
## The Enemies

From the code talkers who had been on the Canal, I also learned more about our enemies. During training it had sometimes seemed as if I was going off to fight monsters, not human beings. But for Bill and Sam, during those first days on Guadalcanal, those enemies were faceless. Zeros swooped in to attack. Sticks of high explosives fell swishing from two-engine bombers, including one old plane that came over every night. Its two engines were so out of sync that its sound was like no other aircraft.

"Everyone called that plane Washing Machine Charlie," Sam said.

Shells landed all around them. Mortars and 75s from enemy batteries. They heard the crack of the .25 caliber rifles of hidden snipers, a sound very different from our own M1s. But they didn't see any Japanese soldiers themselves. At least not alive.

There were plenty of bodies. Taking care of the American dead was the first priority in combat and as a result, the bodies of the Japanese soldiers were often left unburied for days. Those corpses were a fearful thing for Navajos to see. You know, grandchildren, our tradition tells us that we must avoid the bodies of those who have died. A bad spirit sometimes remains around the corpse. To even look upon the body of a dead person may make you sick. If someone dies inside a hogan, that hogan is abandoned forever.

Some white people who knew a little about our beliefs wondered if we'd be able to stand it. Would the Navajos just break down as soon as they actually saw dead people? I admit that it was not easy for us, grandchildren. We did find it deeply disturbing to look on the bodies of the dead, to step over them, even in some sad cases to share a foxhole for a whole night with a slain comrade. But we had been trained as Marines. Long before going into battle, we'd known we'd have to see and even touch the dead. We did our duty.

The enemy soldiers did their duty, too. One of their first duties was to fight to the death. Even if a Japanese soldier was captured and his rifle taken from him, he would still try to attack his captors with a hidden knife. Many years later, after the war, I read a translation of the Imperial Japanese Army Instruction manual. Their warrior's code of Bushido required them to always follow five rules of combat.

1. Obey without question or hesitation.
2. Always take the offensive.
3. Surprise the enemy whenever possible.
4. Never retreat.
5. Never surrender.

Eventually, Sam and Bill told me, a few Japanese prisoners were taken at Guadalcanal. Most were common laborers, not soldiers. They were lower class, uneducated

Japanese who'd been taken from their homes in Japan and forced by their army to work building the air field.

"They were pathetic," Bill McCabe said. "Small men who looked lost and sad. Not monsters at all."

"When we saw them," Sam added, "we realized that our enemies were just human beings."

# CHAPTER FIFTEEN
## Field Maneuvers

Before being shipped to the South Pacific we had to take part in a two-day training exercise on the Big Island of Hawaii. Half of the Big Island is rain forest and the other half is desert, so you could experience all kinds of terrain. Our maneuvers took place out in the desert, which looked very much like our own Dinetah. It even had some of the same plants. Like many of the things that happened to me during the war, that training exercise made me very glad that I was a Navajo.

We had a gung-ho lieutenant. Everybody called him Stormy.

"We're going to see how tough you guys are," he said. "We're going to cross this desert on foot in two days. You've got just one canteen of water each, so you have to make it last. There's no other way you can get water out here."

When he said that, Kee and Bill and Henry and I, the four of us who were Navajos, looked at each other and nodded. We had all seen the clumps of prickly pear cactuses that were growing everywhere.

We started out and it was hot. Pretty soon the other Marines, including the lieutenant, were drinking from their canteens. But not us Navajos. Whenever Stormy wasn't watching, we would cut off a piece of prickly pear cactus, scrape off the spines, and suck out the juice. We knew there was a lot of water inside a prickly pear, even if Stormy didn't have a clue. By night, just about everyone else's canteens were almost empty.

The next day was even hotter. We went about another ten miles and people just wore out.

"Have you guys still got water?" another Marine asked me. I held up my canteen and shook it so he could hear all the water sloshing around.

"How the heck can you get along without water?"

"Oh," I said, "I'm just not thirsty."

"That's just the Indian way," Kee added.

By about 2:00 that afternoon, everybody but us Navajos had collapsed. Stormy was sitting on a little hill.

"Come on," Henry said to him. "We got ten more miles to go."

"You fellas still got water?" he said in a cracked voice.

"Sure," I said, offering my canteen. "Here, Lieutenant, you can have some of mine."

He raised one hand weakly. "No," he said. "That wouldn't be fair." Then he stood up and looked back at his worn-out Marines. "If any of you can't make it, just wait here. I'll have them send back water from camp."

He got about a hundred yards before he fell down. Everybody else fell down right behind him, except us. We four were the only ones standing. Bill tried to help him get up, but he just waved us away.

"Chiefs," Stormy croaked up at us, "do you suppose you guys could go all the way in to camp? I'm going to write a letter for you to take to Colonel Wood asking him to send us out some water."

We did like he said. By the time the water truck got out to them they were all about dead. We never did tell Stormy about prickly pear cactuses. It was more fun having him and the others think that we Navajos were the toughest Marines of all.

A few days after that we shipped out. I was with the Third Division, Ninth Regiment along with several other code talkers, including Bill Toledo. Just as the scuttlebutt had it, we men of the First Marine Amphibious Corps were heading for the Solomons to force a landing on Bougainville. We had to drive out the Japanese and secure the airfields.

We did not go straight into battle, though. First, we had more field maneuvers. This practice was really important. It was to make sure that things did not go wrong too much. I say "too much," grandchildren, because one of the unwritten rules of war is to expect the unexpected. If there's any possible way that something can go wrong, you can bet the ranch that it will. Imagine two dozen ships and a dozen different landing beach sites. Think about all the preliminary air strikes and naval bombardment before even boarding the landing crafts, those LCVPs (short for landing crafts for vehicles and personnel) and LCMs (short for landing crafts, mechanized) that we all just called "alligators." There were also the LSTs, much bigger landing ships that carried tanks and trucks. Then picture 14,000 Marines and 6,000 tons of cargo hitting the beaches by nightfall. Plus, we had to do this against an unknown enemy force dug in and waiting for us with rifles, machine guns, mortars, and artillery. There was no way to avoid foul-ups.

However, practicing a beach landing in a similar setting would help prepare everyone better than just going into a situation cold. So, where did we go to practice? Guadalcanal. From October 17 to 19 of 1943 we conducted landing exercises on the beaches of the Canal. Every Marine who'd be landing on Bougainville felt what it was like to wade through the surf up onto a boiling-hot sandy beach and then stare into the thick mysterious green of a steamy tropical jungle.

Wet and hot. That is what it was everywhere in the Solomons. If I hadn't already been on Hawaii, which had some jungle of its own, it would have been a total shock to me. Think how strange it was for a Navajo boy from a land where rain is so rare that it's a blessing from the Holy People to find himself in a place where it rains every day and sometimes keeps on raining for days on end. Instead of the night songs of the coyote, we would hear the buzzing and chirping and chattering of millions of insects—all of which seemed to see us Marines as their midnight snacks. But they would give us something in return for their meal—malaria.

I had to be careful where I walked and sat. There were leeches and spiders and scorpions everywhere, as well as huge poisonous centipedes. The first one I saw fell from a branch and crawled across my bare arm before flopping off and disappearing into the rotten palm leaves. It left an angry red welt on my skin and my whole arm ached for days after that. There were also giant crocodiles in the swamps and rivers, man-eating sharks and poisonous jellyfish in the ocean. And I did not even want to think about the snakes in that jungle.

There were native people on those islands. They had been there long before the Japanese invaded. Those Solomon Islanders were short, about the same height as us Navajos. Their skins were dark black, almost blue. Their hair was curly and red-red because they dyed it with lime juice. Their teeth were stained red, too, because they were always chewing betel nuts. That dangerous, steamy island was their beloved home. They saw it the way we saw our dry land of Dinetah. It was a sacred place given to them by their gods and they knew how to survive and be happy there. But they had not been happy during the Japanese occupation. Although the Japanese said they were liberating the island, they used the native people like slaves, beating or killing them if they tried to escape.

It was a familiar story to me as a Navajo. It made me feel I had much in common with them. So I spoke more often to the islanders than most white Marines did. Those natives talked a kind of broken English called pidgin, which was not too hard to understand. I remember one man named Gene-gene who was a sort of chief. He had terrible scars all over his chest from when the Japanese had tied him to a tree and tortured him by stabbing him with their bayonets. They'd wanted him to tell them where the American soldiers were, but he'd refused to talk. When night fell, he got loose and crawled to the water. Then, in spite of being weak from the loss of blood, he swam for three miles through water filled with sharks and crocodiles to reach an American Ranger squad and tell them where the Japanese were.

One day, Gene-gene approached me.

"You come," he said.

He took me by the arm and led me to a big rock near the ocean. We sat together there for a time without saying anything. Then he bent over, pressed his palm on the ground, and lifted his hand up to rest it against his chest. I understood. He was telling me this land was in his heart. I knelt down on one knee and did the same, then swung my hand in the direction of the rising sun. Gene-gene nodded. He understood that the land of my own heart was there, far across the wide ocean. He placed his left hand on my chest and I did the same. We stood there like that for a while feeling each other's hearts beat with love for our sacred homelands. It was one of the best conversations I ever had.

For our landing exercise at Guadalcanal, there was a full-scale debarkation of all the equipment and supplies we'd be taking with us when we did it all for real. Bill Toledo and I climbed into a blunt-nosed thirty-six-foot-long Higgins boat with thirty other men and were lowered over the side into the calm sea half a mile off shore. Then we chugged in at six knots an hour toward the tranquil beach.

"Okay," our officers yelled. "Go, go, go!"

My combat pack was on my back, my rifle held at the ready. I jumped in, feeling the warm water fill my boots.

It was strange knowing that American blood had darkened the surf of this island I was landing on so easily. Then my feet sank into the sand. For the first time, I was on soil where American Marines had died fighting the Japanese. I slogged bow-legged up from the beach as quickly as I could through the deep black volcanic sand. I was carrying an eighty-pound TBX radio set strapped to my chest, so I wasn't able to run really fast.

Bill waited for me at the edge of the jungle. I crouched next to him and looked back at the beach. Hundreds of Marines were calmly climbing out of the alligators. Some looked serious, but there was a lot of laughing and joking. Trucks and tanks roared down the ramps of LSTs. Planes buzzed low overhead. There were all the sounds of a full-scale training maneuver. Everything was running like clockwork. Fifty yards farther down the beach George, another code talker and our most experienced radioman, waved at us. Bill and I waved back.

Bill shook his head. "You know what's missing?" he said.

I nodded back at him. What was missing was chaos. There was none of the noise and confusion of real battle. No enemy fire. No bullets striking us, no mortar shells exploding. No wounded men screaming in pain or calling for their mothers. Instead, at one moment when everything was quiet, I heard the haunting cry of a bird echo out from somewhere deep inside the jungle. Our only attackers were a swarm of mosquitoes that descended on me, humming their thirst for my blood.

# CHAPTER SIXTEEN
## Bombardment

One of the strange things about war is the way it brings people together. Before we left Guadalcanal, it reunited me with one of my buddies from basic training. I was standing by the water, looking out at the *President Adams,* the transport ship that would soon carry us to Bougainville. All of a sudden a familiar voice drawled up from behind me.

"Chief, that yew?"

I turned to look at the tall blond-haired, blue-eyed Marine beaming down on me.

"Georgia Boy," I exclaimed, holding out my hand. Instead of shaking it, he picked me up in a bear hug.

"I am so dang glad t' see yew," he said. "I'm gonna be with yew on this here Cartwheel. And I won't let nothin' happen to my little Indian buddy."

"Aside from the four ribs you just broke," I said when he finally put me down and I was able to get my breath back.

But I smiled as I said it. We Navajos know it is always good to see a friend. And it is even better when you know that a friend is going to be by your side in battle.

What was that "Cartwheel" Georgia Boy mentioned? Operation Cartwheel. That's the name they gave the

Allied plan of which our invasion of Bougainville was a part. It was a good name, for our aim was to turn things around. If we succeeded, the Allies would no longer be on the defensive. We would be on the attack.

West of Bougainville were the islands of the Bismarck Archipelego and New Guinea. All of those were in Japanese hands. The biggest and most dangerous Japanese airbase was at Rabaul on the northwest tip of New Britain Island. Every day, Zekes and Vals, Kates and Bettys came streaming out of Rabaul to make life hard for our forces.

Yes, grandchildren, I am sure that now you want to know what Zekes and Vals and Kates and Bettys were. Well, just as we code talkers made up names for things, so, too, did the ordinary fighting men create nicknames for just about everything. They did so for the equipment we used—like the name "alligator" given to our landing boats. And they did so for Japanese planes. Men's names were given to fighters and women's to bombers. Zekes were Zeros, fast little A6M Japanese fighter planes. They could go 700 miles at 350 miles an hour without refueling, and climb up to four miles high in seven minutes. They had two machine guns in the nose, two wing-mounted cannons, and each plane carried a 500-pound bomb. Until our carriers got the new Grumman Hellcats in 1943, nothing in the sky could outfly a Zero. Val was one of the enemy's big, slow two-engine bombers. Kate was the Japanese torpedo-bomber, and Betty was their newer, faster Mitsubishi G4M, a twin-engined long-range bomber.

Why did we make up nicknames? Maybe they were

easier to remember. Maybe, too, they just made frightening things more familiar, even a little funny in the midst of the seriousness of war. Personalizing a submarine that shells your beach every morning by calling it "Oscar" or referring to that one sputtering bomber that flew over Guadalcanal as "Washing Machine Charlie" made them seem less scary. A sense of humor can be just as important for a soldier's survival as a gun or a foxhole.

D-day for Bougainville was November 1, 1943. Thirty-five thousand of the enemy were on the island, but Admiral Halsey and his staff had what they thought was a good plan. Aerial reconaissance had revealed where the main concentrations of Japanese defenders seemed to be—in the southern part of the island. So the best place to attack was on the western shore, a place called Empress Augusta Bay, forty miles from the nearest large Japanese base on Bougainville's other side.

A patrol dropped by a submarine in September had scouted the area and found little evidence of defenses there, although they also reported that the ground was very swampy as soon as you left the beach. There was a Japanese outpost at Cape Torokina nearby, but our scouts thought it had only about a hundred men. Because the terrain was so difficult, with hills and mountains, jungle and swamp, it would be hard for the Japanese to get reinforcements quickly. We could establish a defensible perimeter, build a new airfield, then gradually work our way out to neutralize the whole island.

While we were taking Bougainville, General Mac-Arthur's forces would be landing on the western end of

New Britain Island at Cape Gloucester to establish a new airfield there, too. Planes from the two new fields would have Rabaul caught in between them. MacArthur had wanted to attack Rabaul straight on, but it was heavily defended. Admiral Halsey thought that too many of our boys would die on the beaches. This was before our forces landed on such awful places as Tarawa and Peleliu, Iwo Jima and Okinawa. Our leaders were still innocent about how many American lives it would cost to defeat the determined Japanese.

However, as usual, just as soon as that plan was made, problems began to develop. Admiral Nimitz and the Navy were getting ready for the first attack on the Gilbert Islands, about 2,000 miles northeast of the Solomons. Nimitz demanded some of the battleships and destroyers originally given to Admiral Halsey for our Marines. So, instead of two carrier groups, Halsey now had only one. There was plenty of grumbling in the staff conferences at Guadalcanal about Operation Cartwheel being turned into Operation Shoestring Number Two.

We Marines usually felt resentful toward the Navy, and with good reason. When the first Marines were dropped on Guadalcanal back in August of 1942, the naval commander had been Rear Admiral Richmond Kelly Turner. In one of the dumbest moves of the war, he'd failed to prepare for a Japanese naval attack.

The result was what we Marines called the Battle of the Four Sitting Ducks. On the night of August 8 and 9 a Japanese task force came tearing down the Slot, which is what we called that stretch of ocean between the

Solomon islands and New Britain where the Japanese base at Rabaul was still in operation. They sank four American cruisers. Our whole fire support group was wiped out. Turner was forced to sail away with his supply ships only half unloaded. That left the Marines on Guadalcanal without any naval support, only half of their supplies, and 50,000 Japanese ready to wipe them out. So, with half the spokes knocked out of Operation Cartwheel, lots of Marines were just saying, "Here we go again!"

Few of us slept the night before D-day. We waited on board our ship for the first light of morning to show us the island. I kept checking my watch, uncertain if I wanted its sluggish hands to move faster or just stay still forever. Finally it was 0530—5:30 A.M. in civilian time. The *President Adams* was still a few miles out from land, following the battleships and minesweepers that went ahead of us to enter the bay. Our objective was Blue Beach One, the landing zone closest to Cape Torokina.

It was too dark for me to clearly see the other men around me. Moving through the night sea in enemy waters, our ships were always kept in blackout so they couldn't be seen by Japanese planes. You weren't allowed to light even a match. But I knew that darkness would soon be broken before the dawn. I strained my eyes toward the northeast as I stood by the rail. Other silent men stood watching beside me. We could hear the sound of whetstones being drawn along blades as some of the other Marines sitting on the decks behind us honed their already razor-sharp knives and bayonets. Other leathernecks

were tying and retying their boots, checking and recheck-
ing their packs, their guns, their ammunition.

A few of us tried to carry on conversations, saying anything we could think of to keep ourselves calm.

"What about them Yankees?" said someone with a
southern accent.

I knew it had to be Georgia Boy. He wasn't talking
about northerners. Even though he was from the Deep
South he loved the New York Yankees baseball team.

"They cleaned up them Cardinals four games
straight," Georgia Boy added. No one answered him.

One Marine a few men down to my left was singing
softly to himself the first lines of a song that had just
come out the year before. It was very popular with us
Marines. He had a good voice, but either didn't know the
whole song or was so nervous he could only remember
the first line.

> Praise the Lord and pass the ammunition,
> Praise the Lord and pass the ammunition . . .

I reached down to touch my buckskin pouch filled
with corn pollen. I had prayed earlier that morning, but
now I whispered the words again in our sacred language,
asking the Holy People for protection.

"Get ready for the fireworks, Chief," said the dark
shape of a tall Marine next to me.

Suddenly, a brilliant starburst appeared straight
ahead, followed by another and another. Two seconds
later, the thunder of the cannons reached us. It was 0600.

The destroyer *Wadsworth* had begun the shore bombardment right on schedule. Other bursts of light began to appear as the *Terry* and the *Sigourney* joined in. Each ship had its own fire support area. Their shelling was supposed to soften up the beaches, drive back the enemy, and destroy his positions. It had worked on Guadalcanal. The surprised Japanese there had retreated back from the beaches and the first landings had gone almost unopposed.

Now the last of our minesweeper destroyers, the *Anthony*, opened up. It was so much closer to us that the firing of its big guns outlined the whole ship. The thudding *wha-boom* of its cannons made our own decks quiver. The *Anthony*'s target was a small island called Puruata. Our transports had to pass close by there. The *Anthony*'s five-inchers roared off two-gun salvos, one after another, though no return fire answered.

On and on the shelling went. The whole sea ahead of us was alive with fire and drifting smoke. It was impossible to hear anything other than the constant, deep-thudding booms of our naval bombardment. It was pounding like the giant heart of the war itself or a great thunderstorm without an end.

Bougainville was visible now in the hazy morning light. I saw explosions from shell strikes blossoming on its distant shore. I knew that men might be dying there, but what I saw at that moment did not seem terrible. Those bursts of white fire from the guns, those red circles where shells landed, looked like exotic blossoms, flowers that bloomed, then faded in less than a heartbeat.

The tall Marine standing next to me leaned his head

close to mine. Although I could make out his features now by the light of the explosions, I had never seen him before. He had a little black mustache and thick dark eyebrows that met over his eyes, almost like there was a caterpillar crawling over his brow. His dark eyes gleamed and there was an excited wolfish grin on his face. I've never forgotten that face of his, even though I never saw him again.

"They're giving it to 'em!" he yelled in my ear. "Won't even be a worm left alive on that beach by the time we get there."

I didn't yell anything back to him.

Somehow, I knew his optimistic words were not true. Our naval bombardment went on and on, but I could feel in my bones that there were still enemy soldiers alive on Blue Beach. They were dug deep into the ground in reinforced bunkers. They had not run away from their posts this time. Their hands were on their weapons. They were waiting to kill us.

# CHAPTER SEVENTEEN
## First Landing

All through the bombardment the *President Adams* and the other eleven transport ships kept moving in closer to shore. When we were off Puruata our own guns opened up, firing ranging shots from our three-inch battery. That way if anything came back at us from a shore battery we would have the right range. Nothing came back at us from the island, but our ship's gunners still sprayed it with bursts of twenty-millimeter fire as we passed abeam.

The Marine who'd been singing started up again as soon as we fired our last burst. We were slowly making our way toward our eight landing craft, ready for the signal to board. Apparently our singer was in a different LCVP and so his voice was getting farther away. He'd changed his tune now to one that had just become popular this year.

"Oh what a beautiful morning,
Oh what a beautiful day . . . "
"LAND THE LANDING FORCE."

It was the command everyone had been waiting for. The big chain rattled as our ship dropped anchor. It was 0645. The landing boat I was in jolted back and forth as it was rail-loaded over the side. That is the way we did it then, grandchildren. We'd climb into our landing boats before they were lowered into the water. It made things faster at a time when a few seconds could mean the difference between life and death. Ours was a small landing ship designed for troops, not one of the huge LSTs that carried in trucks and tanks. There were just thirty of us on board.

I sat there. Five minutes passed, then ten. Waiting. Twenty minutes, then half an hour. Waiting and not knowing. Those two things, grandchildren, were always very hard for me. Finally, at 0715, the command was given. We were dropped into the waves and our engines roared. I took a deep breath. We were finally on our way toward the island.

But we were not yet there. Our alligator would not be the first to touch the beach, even though we were in the initial landing wave of 7,000 Marines. Our beach was the farthest away. We were almost three miles from shore and our landing craft only went eight knots an hour. It would take us another ten or fifteen minutes. The longest ten or fifteen minutes I've ever known.

The shelling kept on as we approached the shore, visible in the growing light as a white line of tide. Rounds from our destroyers passed over our heads to strike the beach. Some shots fell short and landed in the sea, raising great columns of water. The sound of our boat's engine changed. We were no longer going forward but holding steady.

"Gotta hold here at five hundred yards," a blocky Marine with lieutenant's stripes shouted back over his shoulder. "Otherwise we might get clobbered by our own shells."

Then, as suddenly as it began, the shelling stopped. The

thunder of the big guns no longer rolled over the water. One final geyser of spray rose ahead of us and that was it. It was like being in a movie theater when the film breaks partway through the show. But we still held off the island.

"That was the main course," said the lieutenant. "Here comes dessert. Fresh fruit delivered by air."

The droning sound that had begun coming from overhead turned into a roar as thirty Grumman TBF Avengers came swooping in. The tubby little fighter planes dove like hornets, bombing and strafing the beaches where we'd soon set foot. Their run only took five minutes. Ammunition spent, bombs dropped, they peeled off, heading back toward their base at Munda.

Some of the Marines on our landing craft cheered.

"Nothing coulda lived through that."

"Home run."

"Bye-bye, Tokyo Joe."

I didn't say anything. I just checked my gear, making sure the radio was strapped tightly in front of me. George Kirk, another code talker who had seen combat on the Canal, had given me that advice about our bulky hand-cranked TBX radios.

"Always carry this big baby right in front of you," he'd said. "It'll protect you from anything short of a mortar round. When it comes to hitting the beach I'd a lot rather have this than one of those new little portable units. Heck, they won't even stop a twenty-two."

"All right," the lieutenant said. "Let's go."

Once again, we moved forward in the waves. It was

bright enough now to see clearly everything in the boat. As I looked back I noticed something I hadn't been able to see before the dark lifted. Our little alligator had a ramp on the back to be lowered when we got close to shore and swung around so the aft side was toward the beach. That way the landing craft could make a quick run back out to sea once everyone was off. Someone with a sense of humor had written words in big letters on that ramp.

FIRE EXIT
WOMEN AND CHILDREN FIRST

We were so close I could see how hard the surf was pounding the shore. The beach was not at all like the one we had practiced on at Guadalcanal. It rose up here from the edge of the water as abruptly as a high wall.

Fifty yards from that steep beach, the guns opened fire. Not ours this time. They were the guns of the Japanese. A round from a Japanese .77 hit the waves so close to us that our boat rocked like a toy swatted by a giant. But we kept going, bullets pinging off the prow.

"Keep your heads down," the lieutenant yelled. "Get ready to go!"

There were eight boats in our wave. As we swung around, I saw the boat to our starboard side take a direct hit. It rose up out of the water in an explosion of smoke and flame and spray. When it fell back it looked as if it had been crushed in a huge fist. Then our ramp grated on the sand.

"GO, GO, GO."

It was not just the lieutenant shouting. We were all yelling that word. And we went.

Someone's hand was on my shoulder as we all surged forward, leaping or stumbling onto the beach, firing our weapons in the directions that it seemed the bullets were coming from, falling onto our bellies to get under the deadly crossfire, crawling up that wall of sand to find ourselves confronted by the jungle's thick walls of green.

Despite all that confusion, the noise of hostile fire, the sound of men crying out as they were hit by shrapnel and bullets, we kept pushing forward. Our training took over, even though some of us were so confused and afraid that we could hardly think. The five boats that survived pulled back from shore to the *President Adams* for another load.

I don't remember digging a foxhole, but I found myself inside one, my shovel stuck in the moist dark sand and tree roots at the bottom of the four-foot-deep hole. The sounds of firing were still all around me as the Japanese continued to cover the beach with their well-planned ambush. Another Marine, close to twice my size, was next to me. I was tying a handkerchief around his arm, which had been wounded by shrapnel. It was Georgia Boy. I hadn't known he was in the landing craft with me, but it must have been his hand on my shoulder, urging me forward as we hit the beach.

"Chief," he said, "y'all are one tough little Navajo. You know y'all drug me in here with one hand?"

I finished knotting the bandage and Georgia Boy leaned back against the wall of our foxhole. As I looked at my watch I noticed that my fingernails were broken and bleeding. It was 0845.

Of the twelve landing zones, our beach, Blue Beach One, was the worst. Despite the sound and fury of our shelling and our air attack, the Japanese pillboxes had been untouched. Dug deep into the coral ten yards back from the beach, roofed with coconut palm logs and concealed under a thatch of leaves, 300 Japanese had waited out the storm. Our hundreds of rounds of five-inch shells had all either landed too short or too far inland or exploded overhead when they hit the palm trees.

I looked back down at Blue Beach One. It was a mess. The surf and the high sand wall had made it impossible to unload the tanks. They were bogged down and stuck. Dozens of landing craft were broached and stranded, some so badly damaged by the surf and the coral reef that they'd have to be towed back for repair.

However, the main concentration of Japanese defenders had been where we made our landing. Everywhere else there had been only light resistance. By nightfall, despite our problems, we had once again managed to bring almost 14,000 Marines and 6,000 tons of equipment on shore.

Our command post was set up at Cape Torokina. Our Navajo net began sending messages from the commanders concerning operational orders. Everything from the rear echelon to the forward echelon and back was sent through us. So I had a clearer picture than most. Seventy Marines killed or missing. Another 124 wounded. The Japanese had resisted hard, but our superior numbers had finally forced them to disappear back into the jungle.

By the late afternoon, everything was as quiet as a picture postcard. It had been a long, strange day. Some of the Solomon Islanders who had been watching our invasion from the jungle came out and began wandering around the beach. They were happy to see us. They shook hands with us Marines and patted us on our shoulders. The natives were all barefoot and almost naked. Some of them carried bows and quivers of arrows.

"Ya'll kill any Japanese with that rig?" Georgia Boy said to one of the islanders whose arrows were tipped with jagged pieces of metal that had once been shrapnel.

The man smiled, showing his red-stained teeth, as he nodded and held up two fingers. Suddenly a mortar shell came whistling in, landed 200 feet away, and exploded. Georgia Boy dove down into our foxhole. The native man, who'd survived months of enemy occupation, didn't even flinch.

He waved his hand. "Him fella bomb fall too far to hurt we. I hear him coming long time. Want fruit?" Then he handed us a bunch of bananas.

As I drifted off to a fitful, exhausted sleep late that night, I thought about what was the strangest thing of all that first day of combat. All that fighting had happened without seeing even one Japanese soldier.

# CHAPTER EIGHTEEN
## On Bougainville

The next two days on Cape Torokina were spent setting up our base and strengthening our position while small parties tried to follow the trails that led farther into the island. It wasn't easy. The jungle was thick and the trails dangerous and narrow. Everything about Bougainville was strange to me. As a Navajo, I was used to a dry land and so were most of the other Marines. Unlike our enemies, our men had never fought in this kind of terrain before.

I quickly discovered that the whole island, aside from the first hundred yards nearest the beach, was nothing but swampy jungle. Whenever I dug another foxhole, cutting down through ferns and rotted vegetation and tree roots and mud, the bottom of it would be filled with water by the time I finished. Whatever wasn't jungle was steep and rugged hills. There was even a volcano on that island and while I was there it was erupting!

I'd read about volcanoes in my geography book and I was excited at the prospect of being so close to a real one. One of the patrols I was on took us so high up on one of those hills that I was above the jungle. And there, only a mile or so away, was the volcano. Boy, that was something. It was all wreathed in smoke from the hot lava inside it.

But the volcano was not the only hot thing on that island. *Everything* was boiling. Bougainville was even steamier than it had been on Guadalcanal. You felt like you were inside a stew pot with the lid on. And although it hardly seemed possible, the insects were fiercer here, too.

"Are the mosquitoes like this where you come from?" I asked Georgia Boy one night as we bedded down, trying to arrange our netting to keep out those buzzing bloodsuckers that always seemed to find ways to get to our skin.

"Well," he drawled, "there's not so many, but there is some big 'uns back home. But if we ties down the horses and cows at night, them mosquitoes don't usually carry 'em off."

Speaking of horses makes me remember the Atabrine pills we had to take to keep from getting malaria. They were big enough to choke a horse and always stuck in my throat when they were going down. They tasted bad and that taste stayed with me for hours after taking them. They were awful.

I hated those pills, so much that I tried to avoid taking them. I would pretend to swallow while hiding the pill under my tongue. That way I could spit it out later. We had a radio tent set up as the base for our communications. Watch Officer Alex Williams was the supervisor there and that was where we went to take our pills. Not only was the watch officer in charge of dispensing the pills to us, he had also been told to keep a very close eye on us Navajos. For some reason we had developed a reputation. So, when he handed me my pill he would watch closely as I put it into my mouth.

"Hold on, Begay," he would say as I started to turn around. "Drink this."

Then he'd hand me a glass of water, stand there in front of me, and watch while I drank the whole thing to make sure the pill actually went down.

Soon, however, I figured out a new way to avoid those awful pills. You know the moccasin game, grandchildren, where we have two teams and one hides the stone, either in one of their hands or in the moccasin, while the other side tries to guess where it is? It is that same game that the ancient animals of the night played long ago against the ancient creatures of the day. If the night creatures won, then there would be darkness all the time on the earth. That was what such creatures of the night as Owl and Bat and Bear wanted. The day creatures wanted night to last only half of the time. Fortunately for us all, Coyote helped the day animals by hiding the stone in his paws so that they won that game. Just like Coyote, I started palming my malaria pill before putting it in my mouth.

It was so much fun trying to trick our watch officer that before long all the other Navajos were doing what I did and not taking their Atabrine. Every code talker would probably have ended up with malaria if Watch Officer Williams had not found out somehow about what we were doing. One day he discovered the pile of pills behind the radio tent where we'd been tossing them. The next day he changed his routine.

"Begay," he barked, "hands at your side and open wide."

Then he put the Atabrine right into my mouth, sticking it as far down my throat as he could reach. I had to stand there until he saw me swallow. Then I had to open my mouth and stick out my tongue. Officer Williams nodded, a grim smile on his face as he moved on to his next Navajo victim.

So our game with Watch Officer Williams and the Atabrine ended with him winning the final round. I suppose, despite how terrible those pills tasted, that I should have been thankful. All the time I was on Bougainville, even though those hungry mosquitoes took half my blood, I never got malaria.

One very sad thing for all us code talkers happened on Cape Torokina. Because the Japanese knew the jungle and we did not, we'd all been ordered to keep close watch as soon as it got dark. That was the time when it was most dangerous. The Japanese liked to attack under the cover of night. Sometimes it would be in force in a banzai attack.

*Banzai* is a word that the Japanese said when they were saluting their emperor, who was sort of like a god to them. It means "ten thousand years." That was how long they thought their new Empire of the Sun would last. In a banzai attack, every Japanese soldier would leave his post and come running at you with a gun or a sword or even just his bare hands. They were also called suicide attacks because that was what it turned out to be for those Japanese soldiers. Thousands and thousands of them died that way during the war, but they also killed and wounded a lot of our men while they were doing it. A banzai attack might come at any time, even in the middle of the night. They would come screaming "Banzai!" at the top of their lungs. They would not stop until you were dead or they were dead.

Other times our enemies would just crawl into a foxhole with a knife, cut someone's throat, and crawl out again. You might wake up to find that the man next to you had been killed that way. The Japanese moved so quietly and stealthily that our code name for them was Na'ats'ǫǫsí. That means "mouse."

Because of the chance of enemy infiltrators we were under orders to never, under any circumstances, leave our wet uncomfortable foxholes after dark. Even if we had to use the latrine.

"That's what your helmets are for," one of our non-coms, Sergeant Wilky, said. And he wasn't joking.

The enemy could be anywhere at night. That was especially the case during those first few days when we had set up our base on Cape Torokina. Anyone seen out of a foxhole would be assumed to be an enemy and could be fired upon.

Just after dawn on the morning of our fourth day on Cape Torokina I was at the command tent when one of our Marine medics rushed in. He was so excited he could barely talk.

"I shot an enemy soldier last night," the medic said. "Right over there."

We went to look and that was when we found Harry Tsosie's body. Harry was one of the code talkers in our group on Bougainville, one of the original twenty-nine.

No one knows why he did it, but he left his foxhole after dark and was mistaken by that medic for the enemy. It was a terrible thing. I don't know if that man who shot him ever forgave himself. His job was to save lives but he'd ended up shooting one of his fellow Marines. Other code talkers died in battle before the end of the war, but Harry Tsosie was the only one killed by friendly fire.

Gradually we extended our beachhead on Bougainville, pushing farther into that wet island. I remember how hard it was to walk. Mud. So much mud. Up to my ankles, up to my knees, even up to my hips. It seemed as if the island were trying to swallow me up. My shoes and socks rotted and fell apart from always being soaked with mud.

Though I had yet to see a live enemy soldier, the Japanese were still there and a constant danger. The first time I saw the body of an enemy soldier was November 7. I was following a trail through the jungle with our squad. The dead man was sitting by the side of the trail, leaning against a coconut tree with his eyes closed as if he was sleeping. I was surprised at how young and peaceful he looked and how small he was. I realized, with a shock, that his face was a lot like that of one of my cousins back home. As I stared at him, there was suddenly a loud *Bang!* from right next to me and one of the buttons on the Japanese soldier's uniform shattered. Sergeant Wilky had fired an M-1 round into the dead man's chest.

"Kill every enemy twice," Wilky said. "Better than gettin' shot by a soldier pretending to be dead."

We continued on down the trail. Ten minutes later, we

heard another gunshot from behind us. Someone in our second squad was killing that enemy soldier a third time.

On November 10 we had a big birthday celebration. It wasn't for a person, but for the Marine Corps itself. Colonel Liversedge, who founded the Third Raider Battalion, spoke about the long tradition of our Marine Corps.

"Men," he said, "it is exactly one hundred and thirty-eight years since the Marines fought in Tripoli and first raised an American flag over foreign soil."

Then he cut the birthday cake with his Marine Corps sword. That cake was four feet tall.

I was sorry that I didn't get to taste the birthday cake. I was so far back in the crowd that it was all gone by the time I got close enough. Maybe I should have said that it was my birthday, too. After ten months of training and combat as a Marine, I was now seventeen years old—according to the records kept by the Indian agent. But I told no one about it. I didn't tell Georgia Boy or any of my white Signal Corps friends, which now included Smitty, the Marine from Boston I'd met during training who'd just been attached to our unit. I sure didn't mention it to other code talkers. Back then, celebrating your birthday was still not a common thing for us Navajos. And after all, November 10 was only the day listed as my birthday. Since my mother remembered my birth as being sometime early on in *Nitch'itsoh*, the month of Big Wind, at Rehoboth School they'd just chosen the date of November 10 at random and made it my birthday.

In honor of the birthday of the Marines, the Second and Third Raider Battalions, who had been in the heaviest fighting, were moved off the front line and allowed to rest for two weeks. However, we code talkers were not given a break. As long as vital secret messages needed to be sent and received, teams of Navajos had to stay by their radios. More LSTs were coming down the Slot between the islands to Bougainville bringing troops, ammo, and fuel. There were always fears that the Japanese would mount more air raids, so all news of shipping in the Slot had to be sent in code. Also, as always, there were urgent messages to be sent in our code when we were out in the field with the enemy close by.

On the very next day, November 11, one of those messages had to be sent. The Ninth Regiment was on the Numa Numa trail, half a mile inland, setting up a new command post. Bill Toledo and I were with them. As we moved down the trail, we saw signs that the Japanese had just retreated. By the side of the trail were weapons, clothing, packs, and other personal items that appeared to have been abandoned in haste. Just about every Marine could be seen picking up equipment and personal items left behind by the enemy as they pulled back. One of the favorite things that we salvaged were the supply packages that were the Japanese equivalent of our cans of C-rations.

C-rations, grandchildren, were the special food packets that we Marines were given to carry with us so that we would have food to eat when we were cut off. Each C-ration package was supposed to be a three-meal-a-day food source. Dry biscuits, canned meat, sugar, and powdered coffee, all in one big can. Sometimes, too, we'd get a D-ration. That was a sort of hard candy bar made out of sugar, chocolate, and oat flour. Every Marine complained about our C-rations. Even though the government kept trying to improve them, nobody loved C-rations. In the last year or so of the war they started giving us something new called K-rations that had a lot more in them, sometimes even fruit drinks, toilet paper, peanuts, and chewing gum. C-rations and K-rations had to be waterproof and able to stand the heat or the cold. So they were backed in tough, wax-coated cardboard. You had to use a knife to cut them open.

Those Japanese food packets were much more interesting than our C-rations. They contained small boxes of Japanese candy, packets of biscuits, cans of stew, as well as lots of pamphlets written in Japanese. A few of us kept those pamphlets as souvenirs but most just threw them away.

However, picking up Japanese things was not wise. Our enemies had learned that American soldiers love to take souvenirs. So the Japanese began to plant booby traps. When one of us tried to pick up a pack or a knife, a supply packet, or even a pen, he might set off an explosion. I had just finished stowing a Japanese food packet in my bag when I heard the sharp sound of an explosion from farther up on the trail. Two Marines had just been wounded in their arms and legs by shrapnel when they tried to retrieve a seemingly discarded .35 caliber Japanese machine pistol.

After sorting out what happened, our lieutenant turned to us code talkers.

"Set up and get ready to send," he ordered as he began to write his message on a pad.

We fastened our radio to a big palm tree and I cranked it up while Bill put on the headphones and picked up the microphone. Then I read off our lieutenant's message to him as I had translated it into our code and written it on my own pad:

> *Da-a a-kha ta-a-tah da-az-jah: Beh Na'ats'ǫǫsí gah-tso dine-ba-whoa-blehi da-n-lei ya-ha-de-tahi tsa-na-dahl nas-nil do ehl-has-teh. Ba-ha-this.*

In English, that meant: To all units: Japanese are booby-trapping personnel equipment, installations, and bivouacs. Over.

*Dine-ba-whoa-blehi,* "man trap," was our word for a booby trap. *Na'ats'ǫǫsí,* "mouse," as I told you already, was the Japanese. If our message had not been sent and received all down the line, I am sure that many of our men would have been wounded or even killed. In fact, as soon as we finished sending and were heading down the trail, I carefully took out the Japanese food pack I'd picked up and tossed it into the jungle.

There were four rules for sending messages in the field: SEND, RECEIVE, ROGER, and MOVE! The Japanese had equipment that could pinpoint where an American radio transmission was coming from. Although they could not decipher our messages, they knew they were important. When they located the source of a Navajo code message, they'd try to take it out. The day Bill Toledo and I relayed that message, the last of those four rules probably saved our lives. No sooner had we shut off the radio, untied it from the tree, and moved, than a Japanese mortar round landed behind us—right where we had been sending and receiving.

Those two months on Bougainville were so hard and strange. It wasn't just the Japanese attacks. The earth itself seemed displeased at the warfare being waged upon it. The deep mud that sucked at our feet, the swarms of insects, the eruptions of the volcano were like messages of the island's unhappiness. On December 6, the whole place began to quiver underfoot like a giant animal trying to shake fleas from its back. I was on a little hill in the jungle with several other Marines looking down on the valley below, which was still in Japanese hands. Until the quake, we'd seen no signs of the enemy. That changed as the ground shook and rolled, and the tall palm trees in the valley began to whip back and forth.

"Look at that!" Smitty said, pointing down into the valley.

Japanese snipers who had been tied in, high up among the palm fronds, were falling out of the tops of those trees like coconuts.

It probably seemed to them, as it did to me, like the end of the world. However, that earthquake ended after only a few moments. Some of the men who had lived in California were used to earthquakes and they laughed at us. But even the California boys did not climb back into their foxholes that night for fear the earth might move again and bury them alive.

The construction battalions, the Seabees, were working hard. In no time at all they'd put up piers, a mess hall, warehouses, and a hospital where there'd been nothing but jungle a few days before. It was amazing what those Seabees could do in such a short time. I really appreciated them, for they made all of our lives a lot easier. Some of the men in the Second Raider Regiment of our Third Marine Division even made a tall wooden sign out of spare planks salvaged from packing crates. They put it where you could see it from the water. It read:

So when we reach
The Isle of Japan
With our caps at a
Jaunty Tilt
We'll enter the city of Tokyo
On the roads the Seabees
Built.

The Seabees also built a base for PT boats on Puruata Island. PTs were fast little patrol boats that were heavily armed. The men who commanded them were the bravest and most reckless boatmen in the Navy. They had no armor at all but relied on their speed and maneuverability in battle. One morning, late in November, two PTs came in escorting a landing craft that had just rescued some Marines who had been trapped on a riverbank.

Another of my white buddies attached to our Signal Corps unit was there with me. Smitty, that same blond Marine from Boston I'd first met at Camp Elliott.

I was seeing a lot of Smitty on Bougainville. Ever since our third day on Cape Torokina, either he or Georgia Boy had been by my side most of the time. Years later I found out that Smitty had a double assignment. His job was not just to serve in our Signal Corps unit, but also to watch over me and protect me—not from the Japanese, but from other Marines who might mistake me for an enemy in disguise because of my brown skin and the sort of Asian look a lot of us Navajos have.

"See that fella there," Smitty said, cocking his thumb at a redheaded lieutenant behind the wheel of one of the PT boats. "His father is Joe Kennedy. His family runs our whole state of Massachusetts, but he's out there risking his life in those motorized egg crates. You know the last boat he was in got sunk? He gets out of this war alive, he'll probably be our next senator. Want to meet him? He likes Indians."

I shook my head. I was shy back then around people I didn't know. So Smitty and I just stood and watched from a distance as that young brown-haired lieutenant climbed out of his boat and went on up the pier to the mess hall without noticing us.

You know, grandchildren, Smitty was right. Just two years later that brown-haired young man was elected to Congress and eventually became president of the United States. So I suppose you could say that John F. Kennedy was the most famous man I almost met. I never visited the White House while JFK was president, for our story was still top secret in those years. I was not invited to Washington to meet the president until many years later.

Things kept moving ahead. The Seabees finished the small airfield at Cape Torokina and were almost done with the bigger one at Piva that would handle bombers. On December 26, the orders were given for the Marines to pack up. We'd established the American presence on the island and pushed the Japanese back. From here on in, Army units would take over. The Doggies wouldn't have it easy, but the hardest part had been done. Air strikes from Bougainville would soon be hitting the main Japanese base at Rabaul so hard that it would be wiped out.

We finally had time to relax. For the first time in weeks we could bathe, get fresh clothing, and sleep without fear of attack. Best of all, mail call brought me a letter from my parents.

Their letter read:

> Dear Son,
>
> All is good with us. We are glad for the pay money you send us. We are all eating well and are in health. We are continually praying in church for your safety and for our other Navajo boys over there. We are praying for your quick return home.

I smiled at the P.S. written at the bottom of the letter. Because my parents could not themselves write English, they had dictated it to my sister, who was now in her sixth year of school.

> P.S. Big brother, I am writing this for our mother and father just as they have said it to me. I wish I could be there with you. School is so boring. I have the same teachers you had and they are just as bad as you said. I can't wait for you to get home and tell me all about your adventures. Then I will not be bored. Return soon.

I would not be returning home soon. I'd already gotten my orders. I had to train for a landing on yet another island. But although I could not go home, I did the next best thing. I packed my unwashed combat fatigues and sent them to my family with a note:

> Dear Parents,
> Here are my clothes, still stained with the sweat and mud and blood of Bougainville. Please use these to stand for me in a protection ceremony.

On the day when prayers and songs would be offered to ask help for me, my clothes would be there, in the hands of my family. On that day I would feel the presence of the Holy People, even though I was an ocean away from my home.

# CHAPTER NINETEEN
## Do You Have a Navajo?

From Bougainville the other code talkers and I went back to Hawaii. There were more changes in our code to make up, learn, and share. Words had to be added for new weapons, military terms, and situations of war. Armored, tracers, napalm . . . Each had to have its equivalent in Navajo. Among those new words was one that we'd grown to know far too well. *Abí zi'aah.* That means "pick 'em off." It was our code word for sniper. Just saying it made me want to duck my head down, remembering my recent experience on Bougainville.

Our Navajo secret code that had begun with a vocabulary of only 265 words was now almost twice that size. Code talkers were in such demand that recruiters were having a hard time finding enough qualified Navajos. Although many commanders had been hesitant at first about trusting Navajos with their most crucial messages, they'd learned to depend on us. Situations in the field had shown our worth.

For example there was the time back on Bougainville when we Marines took a crucial enemy position quicker than anyone expected. Right after our first squad occupied that spot, shells began to hit all around us. Those shells were from our own artillery! This was back before that particular captain in charge was really confident about having an Indian on the radio. I was with them, but they had me carrying a rifle, not a radio. The radioman at the front was not a Navajo, but a white guy named McAdams. McAdams cranked up his set and radioed back: WE ARE AMERICANS! STOP THE ARTILLERY!

But those shells just kept on coming. They'd gotten so many phony messages sent by Japanese soldiers who spoke perfect English that they thought it was just an enemy trick.

McAdams kept begging them to quit shooting us at, but the shells just kept whistling in. Finally, a message was sent back to McAdams from the artillery: DO YOU HAVE A NAVAJO?

"Somebody get Begay up here," the captain yelled. "On the double."

I came running, Smitty right behind me. I handed him my rifle, grabbed hold of the microphone, and started talking code. I no longer remember exactly what I said, but a minute later the shelling stopped. From then on, that captain was sold on us code talkers.

When Marine Corps headquarters asked for recommendations from their generals in the field about the code talker program, the responses were unanimous.

"We need more code talkers now," they said.

Some of the things those generals wrote made me feel so good that I almost laughed out loud. Remember, grandchildren, like so many other Navajos, I had grown up hearing only criticism and hard words from the *bilagáanaas* about our people. We Navajos were stupid.

We were lazy. We could not be taught anything. We could never be as good as any white man. To hear what was now being said truly made the sun shine in my heart.

The Navajos have proved to be excellent Marines, intelligent, industrious, easily taught to send and receive by key and excellent in the field.

That is what the commanding general of the Sixth Marine Division put in his official report. It was recommended that every signal company have eight code talkers. Code talkers should be in every regiment and battalion—from artillery and anti-tank battalions to engineer regiments and scout companies. Each Marine division was expected to have at least 100 code talkers.

On Hawaii, I heard some of what had happened in the campaign to take the far end of New Britain Island so that Rabaul could be under attack from both sides. In the landing at Cape Gloucester and the fighting afterward, our code talkers did a lot. The Navajos on New Britain Island not only sent messages by radio and telephone, sometimes they even carried them by hand, running from one position to another. It was dangerous work, for not only was there the danger of enemy fire, but also the chance that another Marine might mistake a Navajo for an enemy. I was glad that I'd had Smitty and Georgia Boy watching my back on Bougainville. Otherwise what happened to Alex Williams on New Britain Island could have happened to me.

"It was night," Alex said to the group of us sharing stories as we sat looking at the ocean one evening. "There was a heavy rainstorm. The Japanese were attacking and I had to get a message to Second Battalion. Just then, though, wouldn't you know it, my radio went out.

"So I had to take the message to them on foot," Alex continued. "That wasn't so bad, but on my way back I got lost. I was crawling around in the dark trying to find my way when I ran into another Marine. He stared wide-eyed at my face. 'Password,' he growled. The password that night was 'Lame Duck.' So I said it. But he still thought I was a phony. 'You blankety-blank son of a gun,' he snarled. Then he stuck me right in the back with a bayonet. Before it could sink in I rolled headfirst into a foxhole. Luckily I landed on top of Sergeant Curtis, followed close after by that bayonet-wielding jarhead thirsty for my blood. 'What the hell is this?' Sergeant Curtis growled. 'This guy thinks I'm Japanese,' I said. I was glad that Sergeant Curtis was a big man, because I was able to keep him between me and that other Marine." Alex shook his head as he reached to rub his shoulder blade where that bayonet had grazed him. "Sergeant Curtis told the guy I was all right, but I still spent the rest of the night in that foxhole."

At times, while I was back on Hawaii, I felt as if the things around me were not real. It was too quiet and beautiful. There were no guns being fired, no shells exploding around me, no muddy foxholes. I was with other Navajos and we were speaking our sacred language together. I should have been happy, but instead it made me feel ill at ease. I found myself wondering what was happening to Georgia Boy and Smitty. Because they were not Navajos, they had not been sent to Hawaii as I had been. But I no longer thought of them as *bilagáanaa* strangers. They were friends and fellow Marines and I wished they could have enjoyed some of the beauty and peace that was around me at Pearl.

Another of the hard things about being in a war, grandchildren, is that although there are times of quiet when the fighting has stopped, you know you will soon be fighting again. Those quiet times give you the chance to think about what has happened. Some of it you would rather not think about, as you remember the pain and the sorrow. You also have time to worry about what will happen when you go into battle again.

I am sure that is why so many Marines drank heavily when they were in the midst of those quiet times. When they were drunk, they no longer could think of those things. Some of our Navajo code talkers joined in that heavy drinking. After the war, they still kept on with that drinking to try to keep that terrible world of war out of their minds. Never think that war is a good thing, grandchildren. Though it may be necessary at times to defend our people, war is a sickness that must be cured. War is a time out of balance. When it is truly over, we must work to restore peace and sacred harmony once again.

I was not one of those who tried to forget through drinking, although I was tempted. One or two beers or sometimes just a cold bottle of Coca-Cola was enough for me. What helped me through those times of uncertainty were thoughts of my home and family. It comforted me to know that my family was praying for me during those times. I felt close to them when I rose each morning and used corn pollen at dawn. In that way, even when I was sad and afraid, I kept it in mind that the Holy People would not forget me. Being a Navajo and keeping to our Navajo Way helped me survive not just the war, but all those times of quiet and anxious waiting that were not yet peace.

# CHAPTER TWENTY
## The Next Targets

Almost before I knew it, it was June of 1944. The Marianas Islands were the next targets in our island-hopping campaign that had begun at Guadalcanal. The official name for that Marianas campaign was Operation Forager. Our new objectives were Saipan, Tinian, Guam, and Peleliu. They were to be the next stepping stones toward our final destination, Japan itself.

Operation Forager was under the command of Admiral Nimitz, and Marine General Holland Smith was in charge of the amphibious landings. "Howling Mad" Smith was what everyone called him. I met Major General Smith several times during the war. Though he seemed like a mild-mannered man, more like a middle-aged storekeeper than a Marine, I also saw what he looked like when he was angry. His face became red as fire and he seemed to grow twice as tall.

We were divided into two task forces. The Northern Task Force was made up of the Second and Fourth Marine Divisions. The Southern Task Force was made up of the Third Marine Division and the First Army Brigade. I was in that Third Marine Division and found myself reunited with several of my former Signal Corps buddies, including Smitty and Georgia Boy—who once again tried to crack my ribs with one of his southern bear hugs.

"Chief," he drawled, "I am so all-fired glad to see yew."

Smitty pulled back the sleeve of his shirt and held his brown arm next to mine. "Look here," he said, "while our boy Ned has been up in shady Honolulu we've been down here in the sunny South Pacific working on our tans."

Soon, the talk turned to where we were headed. Would it be Saipan or Guam? We didn't have long to wait. Our orders came down the next day. The Northern Task Force would be taking Tinian and Saipan. Our objective was Guam.

All these years later, I am still thankful that I was not sent to Saipan. The other code talkers who landed there all came back alive, but they still do not know how they survived. Their D-day was June 15, 1944. There was much resistance against our first waves that came ashore, and the sea was rough. Boats were tipping over before they even came close to the beach.

Jesse Smith, Wilfred Billey, Danny Akee, Frank Thompson, and Carl Gorman. They were some of the code talkers who landed on Saipan. They said that it was the worst place they had ever been. Of course none of us had yet seen Iwo Jima.

"Shells were hitting the water all around us," Jesse Smith told me later. "Some people had to cut off their packs to keep from drowning and then struggle in to shore without guns or any equipment."

"But when things got a little quieter," Wilfred Billey added, "those of us who lost our stuff were able to go back down to the beach and get packs and guns from the men who got killed and were washed up on shore. There was more than enough."

Saipan was fourteen miles long and five miles wide. Before war came to it, it must have been a beautiful place with its palm trees and sugar plantations. It was the first island the U.S. Marines invaded where there was still a population of Japanese civilians, including many women and children. Having those women and children to defend probably made the Japanese soldiers resist even harder. They fought on the beaches and from caves where their soldiers were dug in. Just as had been the case so many times before, our naval bombardment and air assaults hadn't been very effective in knocking out the coastal defenses. Hundreds of Marines died in the water and on the beaches. As our Marines moved farther inland, the Japanese kept sending wave after wave of banzai attacks against them. But Howling Mad Smith refused to order his Marines to retreat. This is one of the messages that Wilfred Billey sent for General Smith:

*D-ah a-kha t-a-tah da-az-ja: Tses-nah tlo-chin ha-ih-des-ee ma-e ná'áshjaa' gah ne-tah al-tah-je-jay. Le-eh-gade do who-neh bihl-has-ahn.*

To all units: Be on the alert for banzai attacks. Dig in and report positions.

The enemy screamed and threw hand grenades and emptied their weapons as they ran forward. There were thousands of Japanese, soldiers and civilians both, in those attacks. Some were armed with nothing more than sharpened sticks. They believed their only choice was to die for their empire. It is hard to describe how loud and frightening and terrible such attacks are. But all those banzai attacks failed. From dug-in positions, the Marines stopped them with machine gun fire. The enemies fell like tall grass cut by a scythe.

"The saddest part of Saipan," Wilfred told me, "was those Japanese civilians."

The Japanese women and children ran from the Marines in terror. They'd been told that Americans were devils who would kill and torture them. The Japanese government propaganda frightened those poor people so much that they didn't allow themselves to be captured. They blew themselves up with grenades. They climbed to the tops of cliffs and threw their children off before hurling themselves onto the rocks below. Hundreds jumped from the cliffs near Marpi Point or waded into the ocean and drowned before our shocked Marines could reach them. There were tears in Wilfred's eyes as he remembered it.

On Saipan, over 3,000 Americans died between June 15 and July 13, when the Marines were pulled back. The entire Japanese garrison on Saipan of 20,000 men was wiped out. No one knows how many civilians took their own lives.

"There was no way," Wilfred said, "to celebrate after that victory."

Rough as it was, there were still some things we Navajos found to smile about. Danny Akee always seemed to have a funny story to tell, even about D-day on Saipan.

He and Sam Holiday, another of us code talkers, had just finished digging in. Shrapnel was raining down all around them. The ground was shaking from the explosions and they were ducking down. All of a sudden something heavy went *Splat!* right on Danny's helmet.

"I've been hit, I've been hit!" Danny yelled. Then he noticed Sam was looking at his helmet and laughing. What Danny thought was shrapnel was actually a big frog that had jumped into their hole and landed on his helmet.

Then there were the chickens. During the landing, Danny had noticed them flying around.

"That was one of the ways I found out how life is different for an Indian and a white man," Danny said. "Those chickens. You know those C-rations, they were not very good. We might go two or three weeks without a hot meal. But after a while, we see those chickens that belonged to the natives on that island there. So I say to Samuel, 'You make a slingshot.' Samuel, he was a good shot, and he killed one right away. Those white men, they did not know how to make a chicken stew. But we found a big can and boiled water and cut up that chicken and put it in.

"Of course everybody is watching us. 'What you doing, Chief?' they ask us. 'Well, we're gonna make chicken stew.' And we did, you know. We cook it and everyone wants a taste of warm soup there. Even the colonel he said, 'Grab me one, Samuel.' Everybody was boiling chicken soup right around there all day."

# CHAPTER TWENTY-ONE
## Guam

While the Marines of the Second and Fourth Divisions were taking Saipan, our Third Marine Division boarded our own ships and set sail, ready to hit the beaches. The landing on Guam was set for June 18.

But it didn't happen. At the last minute, Admiral Spruance decided to send the Twenty-seventh Army Division, the soldiers who were supposed to be our back-ups, to help take Saipan. The Third Division was ordered to hold their position. The unit I was in was sent back to the little islands of Kwajalein and Eniwetok to the east of Guam. It was hard being told just to wait on those little islands without knowing what was going to happen or when.

"There ain't nothing here tuh do but count legs," Georgia Boy said as we sat in our barracks watching the land crabs scuttling up and down the coconut trees. Those big crabs made me nervous about going out at night. They looked like gigantic spiders and were as common on Eniwetok as ground squirrels are back home. If I ever stepped on one in my bare feet I was sure it would chop my toes off with those big pincers. I was teased about being more scared of crabs than enemy soldiers, but no amount of teasing could get me to set foot out of the barracks after dark, when everyplace outside was crawling with crabs and you could hear them rustling and clicking through the palm leaves.

All there was to do on those islands was drill and swim, play cards and eat fish, complain and sleep. But we were better off bored on shore than stuck on board like the other Marine units. They were kept cooped up on the hot, crowded transport ships out at sea. Stuck there for almost two months, just waiting.

Another strange thing about war, grandchildren, is that when things do not go as planned, they may turn out better. So it was in our invasion of Guam. Our landing was delayed, but not the Navy bombardment. Instead of only one day, they now had almost two weeks to work over the coast of Guam. They were led by Admiral Conolly. Everyone knew him as "Close-up" Conolly and he really lived up to that nickname.

Admiral Conolly had learned from the mistakes at Bougainville and Tarawa where the naval shelling had been too brief or too inaccurate to break down Japanese defenses. Close-up Conolly bought his three cruiser divisions and six battleships in right next to shore to pound the coastal defenses. For thirteen days, the battleships boomed and heavy shells rained down on target. By the time Admiral Conolly was done, the Japanese beach defenses were pulverized. Air strikes had also wiped out all of the Japanese planes on Guam that might have attacked our invading forces.

Finally, we were loaded back on ship and off the shores of Guam.

It meant a lot for us to take Guam. Guam was U.S. territory. Before the Japanese attacked, it had been an American island. I'd read some about it in my geography book in Navajo High School and was reading more about it now. That was one thing that I did before every invasion. I'd scrape up whatever reading matter there was on board ship about the place we were going.

"Begay here is our travel agent," our lieutenant wisecracked. "He's checking out all the best hotels for us to stay in."

Even though they kidded me, the other guys asked me what I'd learned about Guam and I told them. Its people had been American citizens since the Spanish American war. They were called Chamorros. A U.S. Naval base, a deep water harbor, and a Marine airfield had all been taken over by the Japanese when they invaded Guam on December 8, 1941, the day after the attack on Pearl Harbor. The Chamorros had stayed loyal to us after the Japanese came, and they tried to resist. As a result the Japanese had been very cruel to them. If the Chamorros refused to work for the Japanese, they were shot or put into concentration camps on the island.

You know, grandchildren, for a long time even after the war, it was hard for me to have any good thoughts about the Japanese. What troubled me the most was the way they treated the native people of the islands they conquered. They believed only Japanese were real humans. Anyone else could be treated like a dog. Never forget, grandchildren, that we must always see all other people as human beings, worthy of respect. We must never forget, as the Japanese forgot, that all life is holy.

• • • • • • • • • • • • •

"Tumon Bay," Major General Turnage said to his officers as he stood on the bridge. With a wave of his hand he indicated the wide two-and-a-half-mile sweep of beach that was now in view.

Although I was assigned to a landing party, I was up there on the bridge checking signals with the other members of our code team who'd be staying on board to send and receive messages. Because of our special role, we code talkers were often able to go places where ordinary Marines hardly ever set foot.

"Best landing place on the island," Major General Turnage said, nodding his head. "No reef to cross. Nice level sand. Darn fine landing place. Just where the enemy expects us." Then he smiled. "Sorry to disappoint them."

Instead of Tumon Bay, we went farther south. There we would have to cross the reef to land on two western beaches that lay below sheer bluffs. July 21 was set for the invasion, W-day, as our leaders named it. As the first light outlined the island I stood by the rail, watching. I'd managed to find a wooden box to stand on, so I wasn't just looking at the backs of other Marines as sometimes happened.

"Hey, little fella, want me to boost you up on my shoulders?" a familiar voice said from behind me.

It was Smitty, of course. He sometimes kidded me about being so short, but I always had an easy answer: "Bigger guys make bigger targets."

The next thing I knew, I was on an alligator rumbling over the reef. I could hear the roar of the LVT's engines, the whap-whap-whap of small waves hitting the metal side of the boat, and the coral being crushed by the treads, sort of like the sound sugar cubes make when they are crushed between teeth.

But I don't even remember hearing the whistle and the order to land the landing party. Once again, I had that familiar, unsettling feeling of being in a movie where the film has been broken and then spliced together a whole scene later. All of a sudden sand was churning under my feet as I sprinted across the beach. It was easier for me to run now because all us code talkers had the new lighter portable radio units. But it was not just because the new unit on my back was lighter that I ran so much faster. I no longer had forty pounds of TBX radio to hide behind and I needed to get to cover as fast as I could.

Our first wave of alligators had crawled up onto Red Beach just below Asan Point. The beach was small, only 200 yards long, but the bluffs made up for it. They looked like they were ten miles high.

"You got any hills like that back home, Chief?" Smitty yelled.

We had taken shelter in a shell crater from the American bombardment. We'd been met with small arms and machine gun fire, but no enemy bombs or shells were falling among us.

I peered up toward the bluff where he was pointing with his chin. In the time we'd been together he'd learned the Navajo way of pointing with your lips or your chin rather than your hands. That hill rose up steeper than I would have liked. Not really ten miles, but at least

200 feet. We had to climb it, even though the Japanese were firing down at us from the heights.

I looked back toward the shore where a tank was being unloaded.

"As long as we don't have to carry one of those, I think we can do it," I said.

Then we went running across the beach, dodging back and forth so that we would not be a good target for the small arms fire coming from above. All the way up that cliff, bullets kept spraying the sand in our faces and bouncing off the rocks around us. Somehow, neither one of us got hit. But when we got to the top, the fire was so intense that all we could do was dig in along with the rest of the men in our first wave. I got out my radio and began sending. We were going to have to fight for every inch of ground.

It was not easy for us to break out from our beach-head. There were over 18,000 Japanese troops on Guam. They'd mostly been deployed at Tumon Bay, but when their commanders finally realized we weren't going near there, they moved them to head us off and keep us boxed in.

We code talkers were kept busy, sending message after message from the shore to the command ship. Our head-quarters had been set up now on shore and I was told not just to report to the command post but to set myself up a cot there, housed in the same tent as General Howling Mad Smith.

Before long, Admiral Nimitz and his generals were meeting in that tent to discuss battle plans while

we Navajo code talkers waited in the corner, right there next to the top brass. I was only in that tent for a little while, but it made me feel extra safe being guarded right along with the general.

Eventually, though, I was assigned to a unit moving inland. We began to walk our way into the island. It was a slow walk, only a few miles at a time, as we took back the coastal towns of Agat, Asan, and Agana, and pushed through the rice paddies to secure the important road junctions. Every town that we took had been destroyed by the enemy as they retreated.

It made me sad to walk through those broken towns. No living people were to be seen, but there were many bodies of native people, who'd been slaughtered by the angry Japanese as they pulled back. Finally, on July 25, there was a lull in the action and our units were able to regroup.

"Finally," Smitty said, "we can get some rest."

"I don't think so," I said, hoping I was wrong.

But I wasn't. The pause in the fighting did not last. Japanese soldiers had been taught that there was only one thing to do when things were hopeless, when they were surrounded, or when their leaders were killed. Attack. We Marines always began our battles at dawn. The Japanese, though, like the monster beings in our old stories, preferred to strike in the darkness.

The night when the first attack came, some of the men in our group were trying to sleep, but I was not. I just sat staring out into the dark waiting as the slow hours ticked away. Twenty-one hundred hours. Twenty-two hundred

hours. Then, just after midnight, it seemed as if the air grew thick and trembled.

"They are coming," I said, surprised at how calm my voice was.

A single scream, so loud and distorted that it didn't seem to come from a human throat, tore the night. Shapes began hurtling at us out of the darkness amidst the flashing and crashing of weapons and the smell of gunpowder.

We were dug in. Many of those attackers were killed by our machine guns, but others fought their way through. At different places in our line there was hand-to-hand fighting. Each time a wave of attackers was wiped out, another human wave came screaming in. I cannot recall what I did during those hours of darkness, grandchildren. I am glad that my mind does not allow me to remember.

By the time the sun rose the next day, the attacks had ended. Our lines had not been broken. Thirty-five hundred enemy soldiers had died, including many of their high officers. We had not suffered many casualties, but one of them was Johnson Housewood, another of our Navajo code talkers. He'd been with the Twenty-first Marines, dug in on a small hill just a hundred yards past my own foxhole. As he raised his head a bullet had struck him. He was the third code talker to die.

On July 27 we broke out from our beachheads and began to take back the rest of Guam. On August 10 we reached the sea at the north end of the island. There would still be weeks of skirmishing ahead with small groups of enemies still in the hills and jungle, but the battle for Guam was won. As I walked along, the sun was shining and I could feel a little of that sunshine beginning to warm my heart. We trudged down into Agana, the capital city of Guam.

There we set up command posts and a hospital. Little groups of Chamorros who had managed to escape the Japanese began to come back in to Agana. They needed help, but were more eager to help us by telling where the remaining Japanese were hiding.

Because Guam had been an American island for so long, the Chamorros spoke English as well as we did. It was heartbreaking for me to hear their stories and to see the little children whose families were dead. What happened to those Chamorros and the people on the other islands made me think yet again of what had been done to our Navajo people during the time of the Long Walk. I wanted to weep for them. It was just as bad for the Chamorros as it had been for us Indians.

In fact, grandchildren, I think it was worse for the Chamorros. At least we could run to the hills. The people of those little islands had nowhere to get away. Guam was only thirty miles long and seven miles wide. Have you ever had a dream where you see a monster but cannot move your feet to run away? That is how it was for the Chamorros when the Japanese soldiers came.

I tried to do as much as I could, helping them carry their few possessions and sharing my food. Before long, all of us Navajos were bringing the natives right into our chow lines and no one ever objected.

There was one little boy that I will never forget. He was only seven years old and his name was Johnny. His whole family had been killed when the Japanese invaded. Our Navajo way is that no child should ever be without a family. So Wilsie Bitsie brought him into our tent and we gave him a cot to sleep on. He stayed there while we were out on patrol, and he was always waiting for us when we came back, a big smile on his face. He made up a sad little song about what had happened to him.

On the eighth day of December
the Father above
took my father
and took my mother.
He took my sisters
and He took my brothers,
He took Baby Jer,
who was only a month old,
He took them all.
He left me by myself
and I have no one to turn to.

We took care of little Johnny all the time we were on Guam. When we finally got our orders to pull out, leaving him was like losing a member of our family. Wilsie picked little Johnny up and carried him to the Red Cross aid station. They promised they would make sure that he was placed with a good family. The last thing Wilsie did was give Johnny his address back home so that they could always stay in touch by writing to each other.

There is one more story to tell you about Guam, grandchildren. It started out very sad. In those last days of fighting after the Japanese pulled back from the Tiyan airfields on August 7, our patrols pushed their way through the jungle, pursuing them. Charlie Begay, another of our code talkers, was with a forward patrol that walked into an ambush and was cut to pieces. A few hours later, our unit, which included Wilsie and me, discovered what was left of the patrol.

Wilsie found Charlie's body. As he knelt to look at him, I had a hopeless feeling in the pit of my stomach. Charlie's lips were blue and there was no sign of breath. An awful wound, probably from a sword, went from his right shoulder across his neck and chest.

"Graves registration hasn't been through yet," Wilsie said. I could see how upset he was. Charlie had been one of Wilsie's best friends back home. Wilsie took one of Charlie's dog tags and put it into his own pocket. He straightened his friend's body, placed the other dog tag in Charlie's mouth, and tied his mouth shut with a strip of cloth. That was standard procedure to make sure a dead man's identification would not get lost. Then we placed Charlie's body near a log, covered him with leaves and bark, and said a prayer.

Later that day, we gave Charlie's dog tag to the CO, who then packed his belongings, wrote a letter to his family, and sent it all home.

So when Wilsie left Guam he was not just leaving behind little Johnny, but also one of the best friends he'd ever had. We all kept thinking about Charlie's death.

Weeks later, though, back on the Canal, several of us code talkers were sitting around when a jeep pulled up to our tent. I had just gotten back from a little vacation and was being filled in by the guys about what was new. Leslie Cody and I were by the door and Wilsie was on his cot by the tent flap. We all figured they were bringing another Navajo to be Charlie Begay's replacement. I walked up to greet him. But when that person who got out of the jeep turned around, I became speechless. All I could do was stand and stare in shocked silence.

"Have you been to the land of devils?" Leslie Cody said in a hushed voice in Navajo as that person, who now had a little smile on his face, stepped past me into the tent. Like me, Leslie was so shocked he couldn't move.

Wilsie, though, jumped up and ran over to that man. It was Charlie Begay, dressed in clean new khakis.

"*Yáát'eeh,*" Charlie said, his smile getting even broader.

"What happened?" Wilsie stammered. "Last time I saw you, you were dead."

Charlie Begay shook his head and looked down at the ground. "I don't remember much of anything after the Japanese ambushed us. Except I started to feel my feet twitch and then I heard my heart beat. It seems that somebody," he said, looking up at Wilsie, "had put bark and leaves all over me, so I started moving to shake that stuff off. Then when I rolled over I realized some helpful person had stuck my dog tag into my mouth! I was not pleased about that. I was just trying to stand up when graves registration got to me."

Charlie had been evacuated to the hospital ship. He had lost a lot of blood and had a big scar, but eventually was recovered enough to report back for duty. We were all overjoyed that day when Charlie came back to life, and Wilsie was the happiest of us all.

# CHAPTER TWENTY-TWO
## Fatigue

"Look at that thang," Georgia Boy said, pointing at the truck that was one of the "new" vehicles being unloaded for our motor pool. Its dented fenders and worn upholstery were only some of the signs of its age. "I think my grampa done drove it in World War One. Ain't nothin' that us Marines can't patch up, is there?"

I nodded my head and rubbed my sore shoulder. I'd just gotten back from Hawaii. I hadn't been on leave, but in the hospital and I knew just what he meant. He wasn't just talking about trucks.

As always, we Marines in the Pacific got things after the Army was through with them. Most of our tanks and trucks were more than second-hand by the time they reached us. But our mechanics always just patched up the outsides, tuned up the insides, and then repainted them Marine Corps camouflage green.

Truth be told, we Marines were kind of fond of those old used vehicles. We had a lot in common with them. We, too, were always being patched up, dropped somewhere, and told to do the best we could with what we had. And we did it. When we weren't sending or receiving messages, we Navajo code talkers also did what had to be done. If stretcher bearers were needed, we were stretcher bearers. If people were thirsty, we were water carriers.

But those battles took much out of us, grandchildren. We needed time to rest before we were ready to go into combat again. And about the only time we were given even a little vacation was when we'd been hurt in action as I had been.

During the last few days of fighting on Guam, I'd gotten my own chance for one of those little vacations. A few enemy soldiers who refused to give up were still left in the jungle. One of them was a sniper who caught me in his sights.

One moment I had been walking along. The next I heard a sound like the buzzing of an angry bee just as something slapped me on my shoulder. It felt like someone hit me with the palm of his hand, but when I looked at my shoulder I saw blood welling out and felt my knees getting weaker.

"Medic!" somebody was yelling. It took me a minute to realize the voice was Smitty's and that Georgia Boy had picked me up off the ground and was carrying me at a dead run.

I tried to try to make a wisecrack about him mistaking me for a football, but blacked out before I could say it. When I woke up there was a bright light in my eyes and somebody was digging into my shoulder with a scalpel. I was in the operating room on a ship.

I only got a small wound from that bullet. It passed through pretty cleanly without hitting much else before it came out the other side. It was easy for the medic to patch me up. My shoulder hardly even got stiff from it, although I do feel it now on winter nights. It is hardly worth mentioning. I speak of it only to explain why I was forced to head for Hawaii while other men who fought harder than I did carried on.

Not everyone, though, could carry on. Some of the men on the hospital ship with me didn't have any visible wounds, but were badly hurt. They had kept going forward until not just their bodies were worn out but their spirits. They hadn't been physically wounded, but now were unable to do anything. Some just stayed in bed and cried. Some sat up babbling words with no meaning while tearing at their own hair and clothing. Others just stared off into space.

The name the armed forces gave to that sickness of the mind and spirit was "battle fatigue." It was hard for some people to understand, especially those who'd never been in combat. Some even accused those men of being fakers and cowards. But we Navajos understood it well. Our ancestors saw what war does to human beings. When we must fight other humans, injure and kill them, we also injure a part of ourselves. Our spirits become sick from contact with the enemy.

Long, long ago, even the Holy People suffered from this. It happened that way after the Sacred Twins were given the Thunder Bow and the Arrows of Lightning by their father, the Sun. Monster Slayer used those arrows to destroy the monsters that had been devouring the people. He killed the giant Ye'iitsoh. He killed the Monster Who Kicked People off the Cliff, the Horned Monster, the Monster Birds, the Eyes That Kill, the Rolling Rock, and many other awful beings. The only terrible beings that even Monster Slayer was unable to kill were those that still attack us all. Those ones are Poverty, Old Age, and Hunger.

But when Monster Slayer was done with destroying enemies, he became ill himself. Killing those enemies had made him sick. So the first Enemyway ceremony was done to cure him by restoring him to balance.

After Guadalcanal and Bougainville and Guam I, too, felt tired and sick from war. But there was little opportunity for me to give in to fatigue. As soon as my physical wounds were better I was shipped back to the line. More battles lay ahead before any of us could seek the healing of an Enemyway.

That old truck and I belonged to the Marines and we had to go back into battle.

# CHAPTER TWENTY-THREE
## Pavavu

"Happy new year, Jarhead," Smitty said before he poured part of his bottle of beer over my head.

I had to laugh. He and several of our other Signal Corps guys had put on grass skirts and were swaying their hips to imitate the hula dancers we'd been entertained by on Hawaii—which was now thousands of miles away from us poor lonely Marines.

My shoulder was still too stiff for me to lift my arm high enough to return the favor to Smitty, so I covered the mouth of my own bottle of beer with my thumb and shook it.

"Happy 1945," I yelled as I squirted foam back at him.

1945. I could hardly believe it. On the one hand, it seemed to me as if it were a few days ago when I was standing in the recruiting office, convincing the Marines that I was old enough to join up. But on the other hand, remembering the battles I'd been through and the many men I'd seen killed or wounded, it seemed as if those days when I was just a Navajo boy going to school and helping his family with the sheep were long, long ago. I wished so much that this war would be over and I could go back to being just a Navajo sheepherder again.

Along with a lot of other Marines, including a bunch of us code talkers, I was now on a tiny Pacific island called

Pavavu. It was as hot as Bougainville and the bugs were even worse. Not only did a lot of Marines get malaria, there was also this disease carried by insects that made your arms and legs swell up. All we could do was spray DDT everywhere. Yes, grandchildren, I know that DDT is a very bad poison. But back then it was all we had to use. We used so much of it that there was a joke I started making.

"Hey," I'd say to the cooks in the mess hall, "my food didn't taste so good today."

"Next time we'll put more DDT in it."

The DDT didn't stop the rats. They were every-where on Pavavu. Big black and brown rats. After dark the ground rippled with them. If you set foot outside your door at night there was a good chance you would step on one of them. My old friends the giant land crabs were there, too. Just as many of them as there were rats. They were on the ground, climbing up the coconut trees, scratching on the sides of our tents. They never seemed to bother each other, those rats and land crabs, but they sure as shootin' bothered me. As soon as it started to get dark on Pavavu I went inside and stayed there.

But during the days we were kept pretty busy on Pavavu.

"How about *biyaató*? That means 'underwater.'"

"*Chal*, that's frog. That would be good for 'amphibi-ous.'"

As always, we code talkers had to add to our vocabu-lary. Some of the new terms we were creating had to do with secret underwater demolition teams, men trained to swim beneath the surface of the water, with air tanks on their backs and rubber flippers on their feet. They looked so much like underwater monsters that it made me uncomfortable to look at them in their gear. Frogmen.

Those frogmen went quietly at night in small rubber boats into the enemy territory. They did such dangerous things as laying charges on the hulls of enemy ships or placing explosives to clear paths through reefs. We code talkers knew better than anyone what those brave frogmen did, not just because we had to send messages about them. Whenever frogmen teams went in ahead of an invasion, one or two Navajos with radios were with them in their rubber boats. But you can bet that none of us code talkers ever went underwater with them.

Because our code was used for top-secret messages, I knew about a lot of things. I even had heard mention of new giant bombs being prepared. But I told no one. Our code was only one of the many secrets I kept. That was just the way it had to be during wartime. In fact, every serviceman in the Pacific knew secrets that had to be kept from his civilian friends and relatives back in the States. That is why every G.I. letter home was read by censors who often blacked out big sections.

The suicide planes that the Japanese were now sending against us were among those secrets kept from those at home. Japanese pilots were no longer just dropping bombs and strafing. Now they were coming in waves of small planes called kamikazes. Loaded with high explosives, their aim was to dive right into the target, especially big targets like our battleships and aircraft carriers. Before

February of 1945, the ordinary American people didn't know about kamikazes. Our commanders wanted to maintain morale back home and did not want to frighten the civilians. It was like not showing pictures of dead American soldiers. For the whole first year America was in the war, there were no photographs of dead American soldiers in any American newspaper. Not even one until 1943.

It troubled me deeply to think of enemies so determined to kill us that they would give up their own lives. Whenever a Japanese pilot volunteered to become a kamikaze pilot he was given a funeral service before he got into his plane. The Japanese government made it sound as if these men would be great heroes. Their deeds would save Japan.

As I've said before, I have always loved reading history. All through the war, I did research in ship libraries and borrowed books from Marine officers who were history buffs and who liked the idea of an Indian being a historian. I kept on doing that kind of research after the war, too. So, over the years I was able to learn where the idea of the kamikazes came from. Here is the story.

Seven hundred years ago, Kublai Khan was the ruler of China. He decided that he and his Mongols should invade Japan. He put together a huge fleet and sent it off to Japan. But before it got there, a great typhoon roared out of the Pacific and sank every ship. Seven years later, Kublai Khan sent a second huge fleet. Just like the first, it was destroyed by that giant wind that the Japanese began to call Kamikaze. Kamikaze, the holy wind. They believed that holy wind would always defend Japan.

The pilots who flew the suicide missions thought they were flying with that holy wind. A Japanese rear admiral, Masafumi Arima, was the first kamikaze pilot. In October of 1944 he tried to crash his plane into the aircraft carrier *Franklin*. A Navy fighter shot him down into the sea before he was even close. However, the Japanese propaganda machine made him into a martyr. They said that he sank a giant American ship.

Thousands of people volunteered to be kamikaze pilots. Sometimes those planes were so old they could barely take off. Most of them missed. In the Philippines, only one out of every four kamikazes actually struck a target. No big ships were ever sunk by one. However, in Japan, all the newspapers made it sound as if their kamikaze missions were great successes. Soon, they said, the American fleet would be totally destroyed.

What the Japanese newspapers said was far from the truth. Slowly, but surely, the tide had been turned. As the first days of the new year of 1945 turned into weeks, and we sat there waiting on Pavavu, I began to believe that we were close to the end. The Japanese were continuing to retreat. Our planes were now bombing the enemy's homeland. It was clear that Japan was going to be defeated.

"Chief," my friend Smitty said as he read *Stars and Stripes*, the armed forces newspaper given to servicemen. "MacArthur has been kicking butt since he landed at Leyte. Sounds like we're going to be celebrating the Fourth of July in Tokyo this year!"

"Y'all think that's somethin'," Georgia Boy said, holding up the copy of his own paper. My work in teaching him to read had finally paid off a few months earlier. Now hardly a day went by without him wanting to read something aloud to us. "Listen to this here. Mah New York Yankees have been sold to a sny-dee-kat for two million and eight hundred thousand dollahs. That there's about enough to buy the whole state of Georgia."

I nodded to my friends. Each in his own way was excited about the prospect of the war's ending. But from what I now knew about the Japanese, I was very worried. When they decided it was hopeless, what would they do?

Our war in the Pacific was so different from the one fought in Europe. In Europe, when our enemies saw they were losing a battle, they would often surrender. Sometimes tens of thousands of prisoners would be taken. I saw newsreels of long lines of defeated German soldiers, just peacefully walking away from the battle, guarded by only a few Americans. They were abiding by the rules of war. How I wished that the Japanese would behave that way. Their rules, though, were different.

You see, grandchildren, rules about modern warfare were made up between the nations of the world before World War Two. Those rules said that prisoners of war, enemy soldiers who had surrendered or been captured, had to be fed and housed in a humane way. They had to be allowed visits by the Red Cross. Those rules, called the Geneva convention, were agreed to in 1929 and signed by almost every major nation. But not the Japanese. They had different ideas about war. They had been taught since childhood that retreating, surrendering, or being captured in war was a great shame to your nation and family. A Japanese soldier was supposed to die in banzai charges or kill himself rather than give up. Anyone taken captive by the Japanese was scorned as a coward. I learned after the war that as a result of that attitude the Japanese prisoner-of-war camps were terrible places. Captured American and British and Australian soldiers were forced into slave labor, starved, and beaten. Some were even used for medical experiments. Nearly half of the Allied soldiers who were captured by the Japanese during the war died in those camps.

In the years since the war ended I have met former Japanese soldiers. Some even came here to Dinetah and told me they were sorry for the things they did in the war.

"In Japan," one of those former soldiers told me, "the Army had two million men held in reserve along with thousands of kamikaze planes and suicide boats. Twenty-eight million people in our National Reserve Army, some just armed with sharp sticks. Imperial Command told us to prepare for the 'Glorious Death of One Hundred Million' to defend our sacred soil."

Although they were eager to get to Japan, a lot of our military leaders also dreaded that thought. Millions of lives, Japanese and American, would be lost in a full-scale invasion. So our leaders were trying to defeat Japan in other ways.

The first way was through blockades. There were so many people on the Japanese islands that they could not grow enough food to feed everyone. They had to import food, as well as raw materials and fuel. Their fears that they would not have enough to survive as a nation had led them to war so they would be able to control those things they needed. Now their war had cut them off from all their needs. By late 1944, their ships could no longer get into or out of Japan without being attacked by our submarines.

Our other plan was to bomb Japan's cities and factories. If their losses were great enough, perhaps the Japanese command would realize that they had to surrender. Our bombers were flying every day from Saipan and Guam to make raids on Tokyo. First, planes flew over dropping millions of warning leaflets, written in Japanese. *We are going to bomb your city.* Then, after the civilians had been given time to take shelter or leave, the bombers started their runs.

My fear was that neither of those plans would work.

Getting back to Pavavu Island, I have to say there was one thing that took my mind off my fears—being with other Indians, including Navajo friends from back home who were ordinary jarheads and not code talkers. There were about 400 Navajo code talkers, but lots of other Navajos served. Usually, because they were Indians, the Marines put them into scout companies. There were at least one hundred other Navajo Marines in World War Two. Several scout companies were on Pavavu and all of them had Indians. On Pavavu, I met Lakotas, Cheyennes, Cherokees, and Choctaws, even a Zuni.

All of us being Indians in a white man's Marine Corps meant we had a lot in common. For one, every Indian had the same nickname.

"What do the guys in your unit call you?"

The answer was always the same: "They call me Chief."

Sam Little Fingernail, who was Cheyenne, was tired of it.

"We got so many darn chiefs," he said, "there's no room for any Indians."

Sam had a way to respond to people who called him Chief—as long as they weren't superior officers who could bust him for insubordination. When someone who didn't know Sam called him "Chief" he would answer, "What, Mr. President?" Most people got the point.

I never did that, though. I knew that my own white friends who called me Chief didn't mean to insult me and I didn't want to hurt their feelings by correcting them.

We Indians had plenty to share about the things we'd been through—although we Navajos never told any Indian who was not a code talker anything about our secret. Near the end of our time on Pavavu, we all got together and had a sort of powwow. We Navajos did the *Yei'ii Bicheii,* our ceremonial dance that honors the Holy People and brings them into our midst. The Oklahoma boys did some of their dancing, too, and the Zuni guy sang a kind of honoring song for everyone.

That was a good time, but I knew it couldn't last and I was right. Soon after our powwow our orders came to ship out. We were going to Iwo Jima.

# CHAPTER TWENTY-FOUR
# Iwo Jima

Iwo Jima.

"Wull, it looks jes' like a lamb chop," Georgia Boy said, shaking his head.

It was February of 1945 and Central Pacific Command had just sent down its orders to the troops. The biggest Marine force ever assembled was going to assault the Japanese stronghold of Iwo Jima, only 600 miles south of Tokyo.

I'd just shown Georgia Boy the map that pictured the island and he was right. The southern end of Iwo Jima was pointed like the exposed end of a bone. There Mount Suribachi rose 550 feet above the ocean. On top of Mount Suribachi the Japanese had placed big antiaircraft guns to shoot at our bombers. Those guns on the mountaintop were accurate and hit many of our planes.

The flights our new Boeing B-29 bomber planes were now making from the Marianas Islands to Japan and back were very long. It was a 3,000-mile round-trip. The antiaircraft fire was so tough over Japan that many were shot down or so damaged they couldn't make it back to Guam. For the bombing plan to work, we needed an emergency landing field closer to Japan on their way back. Iwo Jima, Admiral Nimitz decided, was the best place for such an emergency landing field. Of course, we Marines were the ones who'd have to take it.

North of Mount Suribachi, the rest of the island widened out. Along the straight area of beach on the southeastern shore of the island was where our Marines would take their first bite of the meat of that "lamb chop." But Iwo Jima would bite back.

The name of our objective had not been mentioned until two weeks before the actual invasion date. In training, it was just called "Island X" or "Workman Island," not Iwo Jima. When I first heard that name, for some reason a cold feeling went down my spine. I wondered if it was because I was going to die there.

Iwo Jima is not a big island. It is only four and a half miles long and two and a half miles wide. Our commanders no longer thought that any small island held by the Japanese would be easy to conquer. But they did believe that what they'd learned from the other island invasions had prepared them for anything our enemies could dish out.

For months, the little volcanic island had been attacked by our planes and bombarded by our ships. But instead of weakening their defenses, it made the Japanese stronger. Tunnels and bunkers, pillboxes and artillery positions were dug even deeper. Big cannons and machine gun nests were hidden in caves and tunnels that couldn't be seen from the air. There were sixteen miles of tunnels on that one small island. Dummy positions, wooden frames covered by sand and rock, were constructed to draw American fire.

The new commander of the island, General Kuribayashi, was determined to fight the Americans in a different way this time. No longer would thousands of Japanese men be thrown at the invading Americans in banzai charges. They wouldn't try to defend the beaches, but would wait instead until the Marines were massed in front of them and then fire from cover. Their new slogan was summed up in General Kuribayashi's "Courageous Battle Vow" that was pasted on the walls of every pillbox.

> Each man will make it his duty
> To kill ten of the enemy before dying.
> Until we are destroyed to the last man,
> We shall harass the enemy. . .

Most of the enemy soldiers now wore white bands around their heads, the same kind of headbands worn by Japanese warriors for hundreds of years. They also wore special cotton waistbands under their clothes and made for each soldier by his wife or his mother or his sisters. They had a special name for those cotton waistbands: *sennimbari*. "Cloth of a Thousand Stitches." They believed that those *sennimbaris* had the power to protect their wearers from being hit by enemy bullets.

Sam Little Fingernail was on the troop ship with us. He'd been sitting behind me sharpening his bayonet and listening as I explained what a *sennimbari* meant to a Japanese soldier.

"Sounds like a ghost shirt," Sam said, a grim smile on his face.

He knew what he was talking about. One of his ancestors was a Lakota Indian who went to fight the U.S. Army wearing a special shirt that was supposed to ward off enemy fire.

"My great-grampa wore one of those when he went against the army," Sam said, the sound of his whetstone against steel punctuating his words. "Go to the Denver Museum, you can see his ghost shirt hanging there. You can even count the holes in it from the bullets that killed him."

The *sennimbaris* didn't work for the Japanese soldiers on Iwo Jima, either. By the end of the battle, more than 20,000 were dead. But so were many of our men.

# CHAPTER TWENTY-FIVE
## In Sight of Suribachi

"Can't be as rough as it was on Tarawa."
"No way as hard as it was taking Peleliu."
"After the Canal, this'll be a piece of cake."

Those are some of the things my Marine buddies said on our way to Iwo Jima. They'd been through the fighting that made those other Pacific Islands feel like little bits of hell on earth. They'd struggled out of sinking landing craft, stormed the beaches while machine gun fire tore up the sand around their feet, heard the terrible sound of air being ripped apart around them by pieces of whirling metal, seen buddies killed right next to them. There was no way this little piece of volcanic garbage could be as bad as what they'd been through.

They were right. Iwo Jima wasn't like those other landings that seemed like bad dreams. It was the worst nightmare of all.

It wasn't the fault of our commanders. Iwo Jima wasn't just "softened up" for a few days before D-day. It was pulverized. For five months, heavy bombs dropped on that little island almost every minute. Hour after hour, for days on end, high explosives poured from the sky like metal rain. It seemed impossible that anything could survive.

What Command didn't know was how deep the enemy

had dug into the island. Those thousands of tons of bombs didn't do much more than disturb the sleep of the Japanese soldiers in reinforced caves and tunnels a hundred feet below the black sand.

They were well-supplied, too. They had distilleries set up to make drinking water and stocks of food enough to last for years. In fact, grandchildren, when we finally took that island and began exploring the deserted Japanese positions, we Marines found something that made us feel especially angry. We were looking through a cave when the beam of my flashlight caught the glint of metal.

"I cannot believe this," I said.

"Wull I'll be danged," Georgia Boy said.

There, stacked from floor to ceiling, were thousands and thousands of boxes of canned goods. There was everything from beans and meat to fruit cocktail—just like those canned goods we Navajos had gotten together on our food drive to help the poor earthquake victims. All of those cases were clearly marked on the side in English: U.S.A. FOOD RELIEF

It was indeed the very same food donated by Americans to Japan before the war. The Japanese military government had stolen it from their own hungry people.

The Fifth Fleet that Admiral Spruance sent in against Iwo Jima was the largest one that had ever sailed the Pacific. Twelve aircraft carriers and forty-four destroyers, forty-four transport ships, thirty minesweepers, and many other vessels. Four hundred sixty-four ships in all. Our fleet was so big that there were four command ships, each with its own team of Navajo code talkers. There were also non-Navajo teams sending and receiving messages in Morse code on the command ships and among the landing forces. However, all the messages sent by Morse code were false, designed to fool any Japanese monitoring our transmissions. Everything important was run through our Navajo net.

The Fifth Marine Amphibious Corps was also the largest landing force in the history of the Marines. Three reinforced divisions, 70,000 men in all. The Fourth and the Fifth would lead the attack.

On February 19, 1945, at about 0100, the major part of our fleet dropped anchor 4,000 yards off the shore of Iwo Jima. Third Division waited fifty miles to the southeast. It would only be called for if it was desperately needed. That need came far sooner than expected.

Breakfast was to be served at about 0500. Before then, though, I made my way quietly to the upper deck. I knew other code talkers were doing the same on the command ships and the other transports.

I stood with nothing over my head but the sky. I faced the east, took a pinch of pollen from my pouch, and placed it on my tongue. I put a little dab of pollen on top of my head and spoke my words to the Holy People.

"Let me have clear thoughts, clear speech, and a good path to walk this day," I prayed as I watched the rising sun.

Breakfast, as always, was a big one. There was a tradition back then of serving every Marine a T-bone steak, eggs and biscuits with lots of gravy, and as much coffee as he could drink before getting onto his landing craft. The idea was that a Marine needed the energy from that food to go into battle.

"Enjoy your last meal, Leatherneck," said the cook who served me.

I smiled and nodded to him. It was part of a ritual our cooks followed. Calling it our last meal was a way of wishing us good luck.

Most Marines ate as much as they could of that big breakfast. But not me. Instead, I took two big slices of bread, stuck my steak in between them, wrapped it up, and stashed it in my combat pack. I had plenty of reasons for doing that. I wasn't feeling hungry yet. Plus, I had seen what happened to a lot of those big breakfasts eaten by keyed-up Marines who had to get into boats being rocked back and forth by the waves. You learned not to stand in front of a jarhead whose face was turning green. His breakfast was about to become fish food.

Another reason for not eating before heading into combat was something no one wanted to talk about. It was better to take a bullet in your guts on an empty stomach. The medics knew that and did what I did—stashed breakfast in their packs or just didn't eat.

My main reason, though, for packing away that steak was that I figured I'd need it later. I'd learned what it was like to be pinned down in a foxhole for hours on end with nothing to chew on but your last C-rations. If that happened on Iwo, I'd be happy to have a steak sandwich in my pack.

As I stood on deck, waiting, ready to climb into the

LST, I got my first look at Iwo Jima appearing in the faint light before dawn. The looming shape of Suribachi made the hair stand up on the back of my neck. That mountain rose like the shadow of a monster against the dark sky.

At 0630, the guns of our support ships began to roar. Fire shot out of the cannons of the *Idaho,* the *Nevada,* the *New York,* and the *Tennessee.* Our bombardment tore up the beaches and the slopes of Suribachi, but there was no answering fire from the shore. Waves of airplanes swept in, Marine Corsair F4Us. They blanketed just about every square foot with rockets and fire. Smoke filled the air, and the hot breeze from the island brought the scent of the napalm to us. But there was no response. It was like the whole island was dead.

Some of us dared to hope that the Japanese defenses had been wiped out by our guns and during the months of bombing. But I remembered the words General Howling Mad Smith spoke at the meeting. He'd been the only commander with serious doubts about the plan.

"This will be the bloodiest fight in Marine Corps history," he said. "We'll catch seven kinds of hell on the beaches and that will be just the beginning. The fighting will be fierce and the casualties will be awful, but my Marines will take the damned island."

My new Signal Corps group was with the first wave. Most of the non-Navajo men were guys I'd just met. Georgia Boy had been assigned to another company in the second wave. Smitty, though, was right beside me. Smitty and I had reached the point where we felt as if we were each other's good luck charm. As long as we stuck together in battle, nothing too bad could happen to either of us.

Our LSTs moved up to the line of departure at 0730 and our amphibious alligators rolled down the ramp into the water. Unlike the first alligators we used on Bougainville, they were more heavily armored all around. Also, each alligator had three machine guns and a seventy-five-millimeter howitzer. After unloading us on the beach, our alligators were supposed to crawl inland another fifty yards to form a line of fire protecting the men who came after us.

0830. The Central Control vessel dipped her pennant. The sixty-eight alligators of our Second Armored Amphibian Battalion crossed the lines of departure. Five minutes behind us was the second wave, then the third, the fourth, the fifth, and the sixth. As so often happened, a nervous Marine behind me started checking his watch and calling out the time.

"Five minutes," he said. Then "Six minutes. . . . Seven."

I could feel it getting warmer as we got closer to the island. Mount Suribachi kept getting larger above us as we continued in.

"Ten minutes. . . . Eleven."

I thought at first that the growing warmth was only nervousness or my imagination as I remembered General Smith's words about hell. But heat actually was coming from the island itself. Iwo Jima had been made by volcanoes. Its name, which means Sulphur Island, is an appropriate one. The closer you got, the hotter it was. When we arrived on the island we'd see cracks in the rock where steam rose up. If you pushed your hand down too far into the loose sand your skin would be burned.

"Fifteen minutes. . . . Sixteen."

At 0906 our alligator ground onto the black sand. The ramp, which had the words WELCOME TO PARADISE printed on it in big block letters, dropped.

"Go," our lieutenant, who was in the boat with us, yelled. "Don't bunch up on the beach."

We poured out, expecting our welcome to be mortars and machine guns. Instead, as our feet sank ankle-deep in the black sand, the only fire we heard was from our own guns out to sea. The four battleships had adjusted their range. The slopes 500 ahead of us were being blanketed with bursting shells that threw up geysers of fiery sand.

Our second wave landed and then our third. There was still no sign of any enemy.

0910.

0915.

0930.

All 9,000 Marines of our first wave were on the beach, ready to move up the steep terraces toward Mount Suribachi and the two airfields on the plateau in the middle of the hilly island.

It had all been too easy. I adjusted the strap of my radio over my shoulder and shook my head as I peered up at the mountain. It seemed to be staring down at me the way a cougar watches a deer before it attacks.

"Hey," Smitty said to me, "this is like a walk in the park, Chief."

Then the Japanese sprung their trap.

# CHAPTER TWENTY-SIX
## The Black Beach

Our Navajo net on board the *Bunker Hill* was set up in the radio room just above the flag bridge at the very top of the ship. It made for a good place to see what happened on the island. Johnny Manuelito told me about it later. As the last boats of our first wave reached the shore, Johnny watched from that flag bridge. He'd just set up to send and receive and was waiting for the first messages. The whole island was blanketed with smoke and dust, but he saw through his binoculars that we'd reached the beaches untouched.

Just then, something came streaking down out of the sky heading right at him. It was a shell from the Japanese guns that had suddenly opened fire. It hit the top deck a few feet below where he was standing. But instead of bursting on impact, it bounced off, went spinning down, ricocheted off the next deck, and blew up far below.

Johnny stared down in silence for a moment. Things like that, he thought, make you feel glad you performed your ceremony. Then he jumped to his radio that had crackled into life as the shores of Iwo Jima burst into flame.

A hundred yards in from the beach, what had seemed like a walk in the park had turned into a swim in a sea of fire. The most intense storm of howitzer and mortar shells, machine gun, and small arms fire any of us had ever experienced was raining down on us. Blue-green vapor lines of Japanese tracer bullets stitched the air above our heads. Once again I heard the sound that is one of the most awful things anyone can hear: the dull thud, between the sound of a slap and a punch, of a bullet hitting the body of a human being. I heard it again and again, followed by cries of pain from those who were not killed when burning pieces of lead struck them.

There was no line of protection between us and the enemy ambush. Our alligators tried to make a quick crawl up the steep slope of the terrace so they could set up a fire line. The black sand was too loose and too deep. Spraying sand, a few of them reached the top of the terrace closest to the beach. But where we were, right below Suribachi, it was just plain impossible. Our amphibious boats turned around, roared back down onto the beach, and churned their way out into the water fifty yards or so. From there, they could at least fire over our heads.

That fifteen-foot rise was just about as hard for a man to climb as for a tracked vehicle. Sand shifted out from under our feet as Smitty and I tried to scramble up the steep slope. My arms were sucked in up to my elbows as I tried to find my balance. Black sand flowed into my face and down my neck.

"Like trying to swim . . . up . . . a waterfall," Smitty grunted as he reached back and grabbed my arm to pull me after him.

I didn't say anything. My mouth was too full of sand. Our work was worth it, though. When we finally reached the top a big reward was waiting for us. Not only did we have a great view, but we were fully exposed to the enemy fire that started the exact instant the two of us got there. The Japanese had waited until we Americans had swarmed up the first slope and were like sitting ducks on the wide plain before the next terrace. Smitty and I fell to our bellies and scrambled like sand lizards to the only cover we could find, a little dip in the ground.

I got out my radio while Smitty dug our foxhole deeper. More Marines were coming in behind us. They needed to know what was happening. I waved at Lieutenant Lewis, who was deepening his own foxhole fifty feet to the right of us. Before long, he had runners bringing me the messages I needed to send back to the ship. Those messages were a measure of how desperate things had become for us by 1100.

Receiving steady fire from grid 29B.
Deliver to Green Beach 1: 5,000 rounds
.30 caliber belted.
Air strikes with 100 pound bombs at 132N.
Estimated battalion casualties, 60 killed.
Two radiomen down.

On board ship, the messages from our Navajo net coordinated gunfire, insured resupply, and helped our commanders estimate what had to be done. Taking the island was going to require every available man. The ships carrying the Third Division were called in.

Many of the things that happened during our first

three days on Iwo Jima are hard for me to remember clearly, grandchildren. That may be just as well. When I think of that time, scattered pictures appear in my mind. Marines running through fire to hurl grenades into pill-boxes. Wounded men limping forward into the fight with nothing more than pistols in their hands. A burning Sherman tank lifted right up into the air and flipped upside down by the explosion of a 500-pound bomb that had been buried as a mine. The still, lifeless faces of men who had shared food with me, laughed and joked only hours before, men whose voices I would never hear again.

Then there were the smells. The odor of sulfur was everywhere. It mixed with the burning gasoline from the flamethrowers and napalm bombs, the sharp tang of gun-powder, the overheated metal of machine gun barrels, so hot that they were melting. Worst of all was the stench of burning skin, so thick at times that many lost their appetites. By the night of that first long day, though, all were so hungry that they wolfed down whatever they had with them. I remember brushing big green flies and black grit off my steak sandwich before eating it in the foxhole Smitty and I constantly had to keep digging out as the hot shifting sand flowed back over our feet.

I also hear clear voices when I remember that time. I hear those voices and my own heart grows calm again. They are Navajo voices speaking strongly in our sacred language. Speaking over the concussions of the exploding shells so close that the pressure in the air made it hard to breathe. Speaking above the deadly whirr of shrapnel, the snap of Japanese rifles, and the ping of bullets bouncing off our radio equipment. Speaking calmly. Speaking even when our enemies tried to confuse us by getting on our frequency to scream loudly in our ears and bang pots and pans.

Speaking. Speaking through that day and the next and the next. Even when our voices grew hoarse, we did not stop. Our Navajo nets kept everything connected like a spider's strands spanning distant branches. The winds of battle never broke our web. As the battle for Iwo Jima raged all around us, our voices held it together.

Our first major objective on the island had been to take Mount Suribachi, but the fierce Japanese resistance made it almost impossible. All we could do was creep forward a few feet at a time. It took us four days to move halfway up the slope, taking terrible casualties all the way.

Friday was the fifth day of fighting. Company E was directed to capture the summit. By now Mount Suribachi's caves and chambers were almost empty. Its blockhouses and pillboxes had been shattered. Howitzers and mortars, naval gunfire, aerial bombing, and men on foot with hand grenades and satchel charges had done their work. Forty men from Company E crawled on their stomachs up the rocky slope that was almost vertical at the top, avoiding any trails for fear they were mined. I was not one of them. I was in a foxhole farther down the mountain, sending progress reports from our lieutenant.

At 1015 the forty men spilled over the side of the cone into the crater. Not one enemy was in sight. The Marines had taken the mountain and as they climbed, one of those guys had found a metal pipe discarded on the slope. They'd brought a small American flag with them. The little flag was fastened to the end of that pipe and the pole was jabbed into the soft soil at the north rim of the crater. Six men raised that flag, including Private Louis Charlo, a Salish Indian Marine from Montana. Sergeant Louis Lowery, a photographer for *Leatherneck* magazine, snapped pictures of the men posing around the flag. Just then, two Japanese soldiers who'd been hidden in a cave attacked them with hand grenades and a sword. Jimmy Robeson, a Marine who'd refused to pose for the picture, shot one of the Japanese soldiers before he could get to the flag and Louis Charlo took care of the other one. Sergeant Lowery's camera was smashed in the fight, but the roll of film inside it was saved and his pictures got printed in *Leatherneck*.

I was too far down the slope to see that flag, but some of the Marines farther up from me saw the Stars and Stripes go up and started shouting and celebrating. Word of that flag-raising flowed down the slope as fast as a stream of sweet water.

One of the white guys in my company yelled over to me from where he was pinned down by enemy fire on the north slope of Motoyama, a ridge in clear view of Suribachi.

"Hey Chief," he shouted, "they raised the Stars and Stripes. It's over, it's all over now."

"Not here," I yelled back to him, ducking as Japanese bullets whizzed over my head.

Teddy Draper was the code talker farthest up the slope

of Mount Suribachi. He couldn't see that flag, either, but his sergeant told him to send the message. So Teddy was the one who first spoke the words in our code, radioing back to General Smith at his command post on the beach. It was a long message because many of the words, such as Suribachi, had to be spelled out.

> *Ashdla-ma-as-tso-si tse-nihl gah tkin neeshch'íí dzeh Ashi-hi, Tkin Tsa-a Ma'ii A-Kha: Belasana Be Mósí. Bi-tsan-dehn ah-ja d-ah naaki naaki tseebii Dzeh Nakia, taa has-clish-nih Táá táí Béésh tigai Lin Klizzie dibeh mósí lin gah tkin ah-jah dah-nas-tsa klesh has-clish-nih gah wóláchíí yeh-hes dibeh ah-nah be-No-da-ih Dibeh Ma'ii ah-jad tsénit klizzie do ye-zhe-al-tsisi-gi Klesh Ah-jah Bi-so-dih Bi-so-dih Tse-noihl neeznaa naaki nos-bas.*

To: 5th Marine Division, Info: ADC
From: LT 228 E Company, Third Platoon
  First Lieutenant H. G. Schrier's platoon raised U.S. flag and secured Mount Suribachi at 1020.

All over the beachhead people greeted the news with cheers and shouts. Having that American flag go up was like New Year's Eve. Some men were so moved that they cried. People were ringing bells, blowing whistles, and sounding horns from the boats. On the beach where so many had died, a man dressed just like every other

Marine got that message and nodded his head. That man knew how hard the other armed forces had tried to terminate the Marines Corps, even while we did the hardest jobs on those islands.

"This means a Marine Corps for the next five hundred years," that man said. He was James Forrestal, the Secretary of the Navy, and he was standing right next to General Howling Mad Smith and two admirals. As far as they were concerned, we had won. But for those of us Marines who were still in the thick of it, the fight for Iwo Jima was far from over.

During that struggle to take Suribachi, three more of our Navajo code talkers ended their war. Paul Kinlahcheeny. Sam Morgan. Willie Notah. When Paul was hit by machine gun fire and died, he called out to Jimmie Gleason, the other Navajo with him.

"Tell my folks," were Paul's last words.

Jimmie got into a foxhole, but was trapped in the crossfire. His ankle had been shattered. He lay there for two days before anyone found him. He ended up losing his leg just below the knee. Jimmy survived to go home, even though the *Gallup Independent* reported that he had been killed in action.

Mount Suribachi was just the southern tip of Iwo Jima, but capturing it meant that we were on our way to winning. Even the Japanese knew they were going to be defeated when they lost their stronghold. I learned later that many of the enemy soldiers wanted to give up, but

were too ashamed to surrender or too afraid of their officers. That was why they fought on until almost every one
of the 20,000 Japanese soldiers was dead. Our victory was
also purchased at an awful cost in American casualties:
6,821 Marines were killed and another 19,207 were
wounded.

During the taking of Iwo Jima, I lost some of my
white buddies, too. I have not said enough about how
many of the white men who fought in the Pacific became my
pals. I had many friends—too many friends. I say "too
many" because having a lot of friends during war can
be a painful thing. It is not like having friends here at
home in peacetime. If you have a good buddy, grandchildren, do you not look forward to seeing him when
each new day dawns? If you have many friends, your life
is full. When you are young and are living in peace, it
seems as if your friends will always be there with you.

It is different in war. Another friend is another person
you might lose at any instant. Each new day, each minute,
may be the last one when you will see your friend. That
guy who shared a canteen of water with you, who teased
you about your fear of snakes, or showed you pictures
of his mother and father, can vanish in one moment as brief
and shocking as a flash of lightning.

It was March 4, before dawn. Three weeks after the
flag-raising on Suribachi. It had been a cold, rainy night.

"Hey, Chief," the man next to me on my left said, his
helmet dripping with water. "Did y'all do another one of
them rain dances?"

It did almost seem as if we Marines were rainmakers.

Wherever we went in the Pacific campaign—Guadalcanal, Bougainville, Guam, Pavavu . . . the rain always seemed to follow us. It was always the same. But there was no confusing where we were now. That harsh odor of Iwo Jima's sulphur smoke was always with us. Imagine the smell that comes just when you strike a match and then think of it filling the air all the time. That is how it was.

Our objective was a place called Hill 362, southwest of Motoyama Village. Although the sun had not risen, we could see it clearly ahead. Harassing fire had been trained on it all night. It was lit up by white phosphorous bursts. Then the shelling stopped. It was 0500, time to move silently through the dark. We were not to fire our weapons until fired upon. That was an easy order for me to observe, grandchildren. I was always so busy with my radio equipment that firing a weapon was the last thing I could do.

As soon as the first light of the sun struck us, so did the enemy. We were raked by fire from our flanks, from the front, and even from the rear. I heard a cry from that man on my left and turned to see my friend Georgia Boy holding his own throat. Blood was spurting through his fingers, and his helmet had been knocked off. A neck wound is bad. The big arteries there have so much pressure that all the blood in your body can be pumped out in a few minutes.

Someone was yelling for a medic. It took me a moment to realize that the person was yelling in Navajo. "Azee'neikáhí." Then I realized I was the one doing the yelling as I pressed my hands down onto Georgia Boy's neck, trying to stem the flow of blood. A corpsman with the small circle of his profession on his helmet knelt by my side. In the Pacific war, our medics did not wear red crosses. The Japanese didn't observe the usual rules of warfare that forbade trying to kill medical personnel. A red cross was just a more visible target for a sniper.

I moved aside as the medic took over. We had to keep moving. My radio was needed farther up front. Georgia Boy's face was pale and his legs were trembling. It was the last I saw of him on Iwo Jima.

On March 16, twenty-six days after D-day, organized resistance was declared at an end. There were still caves and isolated emplacements holding out, but the battle had been won. On March 25, we began withdrawing to head back to Guam. The final thing I remember seeing of Iwo Jima was the American flag still waving from the peak of Mount Suribachi as we sailed away.

You have probably seen that picture taken of six Marines raising the flag on Mount Suribachi. It was published all over the world. You can see it here on this medal. In Washington, D.C., at the Marine Corps memorial, there is a big statue of those Marines raising the flag on Iwo Jima.

But if you remember my description of how Mount Suribachi was taken, you will realize that this flag was not the first one. Two hours after Mount Suribachi was captured, an Associated Press photographer named Joe Rosenthal decided to go up to the top of the mountain, even though everyone told him he was too late. He arrived just at the moment when that first flag was being taken down.

"Colonel Johnson wants to keep this one for a souvenir," he was told. "So we're going to put up a bigger one."

As soon as the first flag was down, Joe Rosenthal began to take pictures of the Marines putting up that second one. One of those pictures became the most famous photograph from World War II. Ira Hayes, a Pima Indian friend of mine from Arizona, is the one farthest on the very left. You can see him reaching for the flagpole but not quite touching it. He and the other five became famous because of that one photograph. It embarrassed some of them, because they all knew it was a replacement flag.

I think that even though there was no fighting on top of Mount Suribachi at that time, those six men deserved the praise they were given. They were brave and fought hard. Three of them were killed not long after that photograph. The other three, including Ira, were shipped back to the States. Ira toured the country for the Marine Corps, promoting the sale of war bonds.

When they made Ira into a celebrity, he didn't feel comfortable about it. I think that's one of the reasons he drank so much. Some of us, like Wilsie Bitsie and me, had been friends with Ira even before the war. So we Navajos saw a lot of Ira after he got back home, all of us being veterans and back in Arizona. All of us being Indians. Ira would tell us how he just couldn't get the war out of his head. He kept seeing the men who had been wounded and hearing their voices. He didn't like to look at that famous photo of himself raising the flag.

"I wish you had been there with me in that picture," he used to say to Wilsie and me. "It is so lonely being there forever without another Indian."

# CHAPTER TWENTY-SEVEN
# Okinawa

Iwo Jima was the key. It opened the door to the invasion of Japan and the end of the Pacific War. B-29s from Guam and Saipan passed over Iwo Jima without being attacked. Dozens and dozens of planes used Sulphur Island as an emergency landing field on their way back from bombing Japan.

On the islands of Japan, many people wished the war to end. There were plenty of people who hadn't wanted their country to go to war with the United States. As more of their loved ones died on faraway islands, many Japanese people saw that nothing was possible but defeat. The Imperial Command, however, was still led by military men who refused to accept surrender. The war had to go on.

So, once again, we code talkers took part in another invasion. About fifty of us were part of the operation. We were called Operation Iceberg. Our 1,600 ships were the largest armada in history, and the number of our troops was even bigger than the force that landed on the beaches of Normandy in Europe. I was now with the Sixth Division, made up of regiments from other disbanded divisions. This time we were to invade the island of Okinawa, even closer to Japan. The Okinawan people had always been peaceful and had no history of ever going to war. But when the Japanese took over their island, our enemies made it into another military fortress.

Our carriers went first, sending planes against the Okinawan airfields. Many enemy aircraft were destroyed on the grounds, but others took off to attack our ships. Kamikaze planes fell out of the sky toward our carriers. Those swarms of small planes looked to me like wasps whose nest has been poked by a stick. Many were shot down and just as many fell into the sea without hitting any target. A lot of those planes were piloted by young men who'd never flown before. They were allowed to get drunk before taking off, since it would be their last drink.

Too many of those planes did strike their targets. The *Hornet* and the *Franklin* were hit the hardest. Over 700 men died on the *Franklin*. I saw it burning right next to me as our invasion force steamed on. In addition to my Navajo buddies two of my white friends who had survived the other campaigns were there with me. Of course, one of them was Smitty, who was stuck to my side like a burr. Who was the other one?

One of the greatest surprises I have ever had in my life came just after we left port for Okinawa. As I stood by the rail, a familiar drawling voice spoke up next to me.

"Hey Chief, what y'all gonna do when y'all see one of them habu snakes? I hear they's just a-crawlin' all over Okinawa."

It was Georgia Boy. He had survived his wounds.

There was a big bandage on his neck, but an even bigger smile on his face.

I hugged him so hard that for once I was the one who lifted him off his feet and almost cracked his ribs. Then the deck shifted as the ship turned and we both almost went over the rail. Smitty, though, grabbed us and pulled us back. The three of us stood there laughing our heads off.

"Why aren't you dead, you good-for-nothing redneck?" Smitty said.

"Can't kill a cracker with just one little Jap bullet," Georgia Boy answered, grinning.

We weren't the only ones grinning. The mood on board our ships was really good. Even Radio Tokyo, still broadcasting its usual mixture of American music, bold-faced lies, and threats, brought a smile to most people's faces.

> This is the zero hour, boys. It is broadcast for all you American fighting men in the Pacific, particularly those standing off the shores of Okinawa because many of you will never hear another program. Here's a nice number for you, "Going Home." It's nice work if you can get it.

There was a time when ominous words like those from Tokyo Rose had made the hair stand up on the back of my neck. Now those broadcasts just amused me. Most of us Marines were spending more time joking and talking about how the war had to end soon than worrying about the impending battle.

"What are you going to do when you get home, Chief?" Smitty asked me.

"He's gonna eat mutton," Georgia Boy said, chuckling.

"Me," Smitty said, "I'm going back to college. That G.I. Bill is going to give me a free education."

I didn't answer them. Much as I wanted to go home, deep in my heart it was still hard for me to believe that the war was almost over. Okinawa still lay ahead of us, and then the other islands of Japan.

April 1 was landing day on Okinawa. It was also Easter Sunday. One hundred fifty-four thousand of us G.I.s and Marines were poised to hit the Hagushi beaches. As I climbed into the boat, my stomach felt tight as a drum. Would this be like it was on Iwo Jima? Once again, as the boat powered through the waves, there was no enemy fire at all. All that greeted me as I stepped out onto the rocky shore was a gentle wind. I dreaded what would happen next. Would it be another ambush as soon as enough of us were ashore? But as more and more men came out of the water there was still no resistance at all. Hour after hour passed. The only thing that broke the quiet was the roar of amphibious tanks. Before long, all of us were calling that day by a new name.

"This ain't landing day," Georgia Boy said as we sat watching more and more troops and equipment follow us up onto the beach. "This here is love day. Taking this here place gonna be as easy for us as it was for mah Yankees to win the series in '43."

"Hey, Georgia Boy," Smitty said, "you ever hear this song?" Then he began whistling "Meet Me in St. Louis."

It made us all chuckle, even Georgia Boy. That past October, the Yankees had not even made it to the World Series. It turned out to be a Missouri special, with the St. Louis Cardinals winning in four over the St. Louis Browns.

By nightfall, we'd already reached objectives that were supposed to have taken days. Bulldozers were clearing away the wreckage of Japanese planes on Yontan airfield. It all seemed too easy. And it was.

On April 8 we hit Kakazu Ridge. The Japanese soldiers had pulled back and dug in to wait for us. Their first line of defense was a long rocky ridge, heavily fortified, but so camouflaged that we didn't know it was there. Their plan was to hold us off at their defense lines, to be the rock that would break the sword of our attack. The Japanese Imperial general headquarters wanted to bleed us white. They hoped that so many Americans would die we'd lose heart and stop our attacks. That was the idea of one of their best military men, General Ushijima, and it almost worked.

I don't mean that we almost gave up, but it took a long time and we lost so many good men. Our battle for Okinawa was some of the bloodiest fighting in the war. It was made even harder because there were no good roads and the island was crossed by ranges of hills running from east to west. We had to fight from one ridge to the next. It seemed it would never end.

I have spoken so much about other battles I saw, that I will say little more about Okinawa than that it took us eighty-three days. The island was finally declared secure on June 2, 1945. On that same day, General Ushijima committed suicide. Twelve thousand Americans were dead or missing. Thirty-six of our smaller ships had been sunk by the kamikazes and about four hundred more had been damaged by the attacks. The Japanese had lost 3,600 airplanes and 110,000 men. Eighty thousand Okinawan civilians also died in the battles. Through it all our Navajo code was used to send and receive messages. We Navajos had helped a lot, but rather than feeling glad about it, I had a great heaviness in my heart.

If it cost this much to take just one small island, invading the big islands of Japan would be too terrible to imagine. Our commanders now estimated there'd be at least one million American casualties. No one knew how many Japanese soldiers and civilians would die. Thousands of kamikaze planes, suicide boats, human torpedoes, and midget submarines had been prepared by our enemies. Tens of millions of Japanese would give their lives to defend their homeland. All our intelligence said that the Japanese military was still not ready to quit, even though the ordinary people were desperate for peace.

Although I did not know it at the time, grandchildren, all through the war many Japanese citizens were imprisoned or murdered because they spoke out against it. There was a powerful military organization called the Thought Police in Japan. If you were suspected of even thinking about criticizing the government, you'd be taken away by the Thought Police. It was also hard for the Japanese to speak up because they believed that their emperor was a god, the son of the Sun God. They had to do what they were told because their emperor could do no wrong.

Some brave Japanese people tried to let their emperor know how they felt. There were some men whose sons had died during the war who chose a certain way to tell their emperor there had been enough sacrifice. They did so through a sacrifice of their own. First it was only a few, but by the last year of the war, there were many. Each grieving father sent a small package, carefully wrapped, to the Imperial palace. None of those packages ever reached the emperor. They were quickly disposed of by men who'd been appointed to keep all bad news from reaching Emperor Hirohito. Each package contained the sender's right index finger.

It seems that Emperor Hirohito did not know what was truly happening much of the time. Any Japanese defeat was too embarrassing for the military leaders to admit to their immediate superiors, much less to their divine emperor. The real power in Japan during World War Two was held by the Supreme Military Council, who assured the emperor that their decisions were best for their nation. While we kept secrets from our enemies, our enemies kept secrets from each other, lying to their own people about what was truly happening.

One of the saddest messages we code talkers ever received came on April 12, 1945. As soon as I got it on my radio, I took off my headphones. I couldn't talk. My throat was choked up and my eyes were filled with tears.

Johnny Manuelito was my partner in the radio room that day. He put his hand on my shoulder.

"What is it?" he asked.

"Our FDR is gone," I finally managed to answer in a choked voice. "The president of the United States has died."

It was a great shock to everyone. Few people knew how sick President Franklin Delano Roosevelt had been. Now everybody knows too much about everyone, even the personal lives of our leaders. Back then, though, things like that were kept private. Many Americans did not even know President Roosevelt was crippled by polio. Roosevelt had been our president for more than three terms in office. People loved and trusted him. On the decks of ships and the shores of Pacific islands, Marines, sailors, and soldiers knelt and wept together in prayer services for our fallen president. That morning, when I offered pollen, I prayed for his family and those who loved him.

I will tell you one story about Okinawa, grandchildren. It is one of my best memories of the whole war. A group of us code talkers had been able to catch a goat. We butchered it and cooked it over a fire. It was almost as good as mutton. Its smell brought other Indians. One of them was my Cheyenne buddy from Iwo Jima, Sam

Little Fingernail, who was now a scout with the Sixth. As he cut off a piece of that goat he began to smile.

"This makes me think of a story my Lakota great-grampa told me," he said. "He was in the big fight when we wiped out Custer. But halfway through the battle, he rode over a hill and there were two other Lakotas sitting around a fire cooking meat. They had just killed a buffalo. So the three of them sat around eating buffalo steak before going back into the fight."

"Good story," I said. "Now pass me some of that buffalo mutton." We all laughed and laughed.

For a time, on that faraway island, we were just Indians sitting around a fire and eating. It was like the old days, long before any white man's war.

# CHAPTER TWENTY-EIGHT
## The Bomb

The Allied plan of bombing the great cities of the Japanese mainland had continued all through our invasion of Okinawa. From high in the sky B-29s dropped thousands of tons of high explosives on every Japanese city. Toyko itself was completely destroyed in a giant firestorm. In July of 1945, Emperor Hirohito sent a letter to the Supreme Military Council, urging them to seek peace. They ignored his message.

Then, on August 6, 1945, a plane took off from the air base on Saipan. It carried America's secret weapon, a single atomic bomb. When that bomb fell on Hiroshima, it destroyed the whole city. Over 70,000 people died. Two days later, a second plane took off from Tinian and dropped a second atomic bomb on Nagasaki.

Until then, Emperor Hirohito had not spoken directly in the Supreme Council. But this news was too much for him. He went to the council in person.

"I swallow my own tears," he said, "and give my sanction to the Allied proposal."

Although the Japanese emperor was ready to offer unconditional surrender, not all of the military officers agreed. There was even an attempted coup, but it failed. Finally, on August 15, Emperor Hirohito spoke over the radio to the Japanese people, telling them that Japan was surrendering. It was a shock to those people in many ways, grandchildren. None of them had ever expected to personally hear their emperor. Remember that Hirohito was a distant god to them. They had never heard a god's voice before.

Of course, we code talkers were the first to receive the message that Japan had surrendered. It came over division radio early that night. Emperor Hirohito was asking for peace terms. I was so excited that I stood up and started shouting. Several of us Navajos were there by the radio and we could hardly believe it. I stuck my head out of the tent.

"War is over," I shouted to the other Marines. "Japan is surrendering."

Then we Navajos tore off our shirts and began dancing around. We headed right for the bandsmen's tents, where we liberated some of their little drums. Each one of us code talkers grabbed a drum and we went dancing down the road, beating on those drums, yelling and singing in Navajo. Some of the other Marines who watched us shook their heads, while others joined in or celebrated in their own way. I think everyone had a smile on his face.

How happy we all were. One minute we had all been at war and then the next it was over. There would be no more killing. I would be able to return to my beloved home.

Ah, that was such a good night, grandchildren.

# CHAPTER TWENTY-NINE
## Going Home

It turned out that none of us code talkers could go home as soon as the end of the war was announced. There was still work for us to do. Two Navajo code talkers, Paul Blatchford and Rex Malone, were reassigned to Army and Navy Intelligence and shipped out with special teams to Japan to visit Hiroshima and Nagasaki ahead of our troops. They sent their reports back to San Francisco in Navajo code where others of us had been sent. I was one of those in San Francisco who received their messages. Those messages shocked me.

Paul and Rex were horrified at what they saw where our two atomic bombs had fallen. All the buildings were flat and burned. Pitiful, injured survivors were camping out in sheds made from pine trees. Those sheds looked to Paul and Rex just like the lean-tos made back home by our own Navajo people. Many of those Japanese survivors looked so Indian that they might have been Navajos. They said it was hard to look at those people and think of them as enemies.

Our leaders all told us that those atomic bombs were needed to end the war. That may have been so, grandchildren. I have no doubt that they made the war shorter. However, receiving those messages made me pray hard that such bombs would never fall on human beings again.

A few of our number never left the Marines at all. They decided it would be a good career for them and re-enlisted. Among them were Bill Kien, Bill Price, and Dean Wilson. They became twenty-year men. Others joined different branches of the armed forces. Later on, in Korea and in Vietnam, Navajos would again use our code to send secret messages in battles. Some code talkers stayed on in the Pacific after they were discharged. They had discovered when they were in New Zealand and in Australia that they were not treated badly because they were Indians, but respected as Americans who fought in the war. They married local girls and just stayed there for the rest of their lives. Most of us, though, eventually got back here to Dinetah, just as I did when my tour of duty finally ended.

Before we left the Marines, each of us was sternly reminded that our code was still a top secret. We could not talk with anyone about it. It was so secret that our real "occupational specialty" was not even mentioned on our discharge papers. Usually, a Marine's discharge papers indicate what he was trained to do. Sometimes those were professions that were needed back home. Having it on your discharge that you had been a mechanic or an electrician or a radio operator could help you get a job. There was a special number for each type of work in *The United States Marine Corps Manual of Military Occupational Specialties*. Our number was 642.

642 code talker: Transmits and receives mes-sages in a restricted language by radio and

wire. Sends and receives messages by means of semaphores and other visual signals. May perform field lineman, switchboard operator, or other communication duties.

But that number 642 was not on my discharge or on the papers of other code talkers. As far as the outside world was concerned, I had just been an ordinary Marine with no specialty at all.

"You can't tell anyone about what you really did, Marine," my commanding officer said to me. Then he smiled. It was a grim smile with no humor in it. "But you'll probably be hearing from us soon. We may be at war with the Russians in another year or so. You fellows will certainly be needed again then."

I prayed it would not be so and I am thankful that war with Russia never came to be.

Some of us were not sure what we would do when we got home, and I was one of them. I sat in the bus that went from California to Arizona, just watching the miles go by. It was as if I were in a dream. After all our hardships in the Pacific war, things felt too easy now. Nothing around me seemed real. Then something happened to me that was all too real and it showed me what I had to do.

I had just gotten off the bus in a little town at the edge of our reservation. I was feeling thirsty. So I went into a bar to get a Coke. I was still wearing my uniform. While I'd been in San Francisco and I wore my uniform in the street, people of all kinds would come up to me and say hello. Some would shake my hand and thank me for fighting for our country. Now that I was almost home it was different.

The bartender, a big *bilagáanaa* with a red, sweaty face, glared at me.

"Can't you read, you stupid Navajo?" he said, pointing at a sign hung over the bar. It said NO INDIANS SERVED HERE. Two other white customers along the bar glared at me as I read the sign aloud.

"I don't want an Indian," I said. "I'm just a thirsty Marine who wants a Coke."

They didn't laugh at my joke. The bartender and the two other white men just grabbed me and threw me out into the street. I did not try to fight them. Even though I was small, I was strong and I had been trained as a Marine. I could have given them a real fight. But I understood it would not accomplish anything. I walked away, having realized something.

Although I had changed, the things that had made me feel sad and ashamed when I was a child in boarding school had stayed the same. It didn't matter that I had fought for America. It didn't matter that I had made white friends who would have sacrificed their lives to save me when we were at war. In the eyes of those prejudiced *bilagáanaas* in that bar, I was just another stupid Navajo.

But I did not walk away thinking that things were hopeless. I did not try to find a bar that would sell an Indian liquor so that I could lose my sorrows by drinking. I had learned to be self-confident as a Marine, to believe that I could succeed even in the hardest battle.

Now I had another battle ahead of me, one that could be fought in another way.

I could go back and finish my last year of high school. I could take advantage of that G.I. Bill the other Marines had spoken about. I could go on to college and become a teacher. I could learn how to teach our language to our children. I could also learn more about history so that I could understand things and help our children to understand by reminding them to never forget our language and our culture. And that is what I did.

It was not easy and I did not do it quickly. For one thing, I still had to be healed. Those of us who came back to Dinetah from the war were all wounded, not just in our bodies, but in our minds and our spirits. You know that our Navajo way is to be quiet and modest. So when we Navajo soldiers came back, there were no parties or big parades for us as there were for the *bilagáanaa* G.I.s in their hometowns. We Navajos were just expected to fit back in.

I began to have awful nightmares. I woke up from seeing men die and hearing the sounds of their cries. Exploding shells burst in my dreams as wave after wave of screaming enemy soldiers came at me.

But although I had no victory parades, I had something else. I had my family and our traditional ceremonies. I had the Holy People to help me. Finally, when it seemed I was about to go crazy, my family insisted that I have an Enemyway. My old friend Hosteen Mitchell made all the arrangements and the ceremony was done for me.

It brought me back into balance. I know just the moment when that happened. It was during the first night of my Enemyway when everything was quiet. As I was sitting and waiting for the next part of the ceremony to begin I closed my eyes and I was back on Bougainville.

It was night on the island. We were surrounded by the enemy. Smitty was sound asleep beside me. Then I heard singing in Navajo. Was I awake or dreaming? I floated out of my foxhole, right into the jungle. The moonlight was bright and everything around me that had seemed strange and threatening was now beautiful. Every leaf, every flower, every small creature that crawled or flew was beautiful. Even the leeches and mosquitoes that wanted to suck my blood, even the land crabs whose shells sparkled like turquoise in the moonlight no longer seemed alien to me. Everything was just the way it should be and all was in perfect balance. Then someone was shaking my shoulder. I was back in the foxhole. It was morning. Smitty was telling me the Japanese were gone. They had pulled back. We were safe.

I closed my eyes in relief and heard that singing voice in Navajo again. This time when I opened my eyes, I was home, truly home. Big Schoolboy was shaking his rattle and I was at peace. My balance had been restored. I could go forward on a path of beauty.

Through all the years that we kept our secret about having been code talkers, I worked hard for our people as a teacher and a member of our community. All around me

I saw other code talkers doing the same, each in his own way. Some went to colleges and universities and training schools. Some became engineers or business owners or artists. It was not easy. In some ways that G.I. Bill was not fair to us Navajos. Other ex-servicemen could use it to help them build or buy their own homes, but not us.

Smitty and Georgia Boy both sent me photos of their new homes. I wrote back and congratulated them without telling them that I could never do what they had done. It didn't work that way for Indians. Because the houses we wanted to build would be on Indian reservations, we were refused help. We could only build or buy a home outside of our sacred homeland. Just like many other things in the *bilagáanaa* world, that housing rule was unfair to Indians.

However, I never gave up. I just became more determined. I took part in tribal government, working for education reform on our reservation. Although I did not accomplish as much as I had hoped, I am proud of the things that I did over the years.

Finally, in 1969, we were told that we could speak about being code talkers. New computers were more efficient than people in sending and receiving code. Our story was declassified. We formed a Code Talkers Association and began having meetings. Books were written about us and we were invited to speak at special events. We were invited to the White House by one president after another. We were given medals like this one.

All of that was good, grandchildren. But more important than any praise was the fact that we could now tell this story. We could tell our children and our grandchildren about the way our sacred language helped this country.

So, my grandchildren, that is the tale this medal has helped me to tell. It is not just my story, but a story of our people and of the strength that we gain from holding on to our language, from being Dine'. I pray that none of you will ever have to go into battle as I did. I also pray that you will fight to keep our language, to hold on to it with the same warrior spirit that our Indian people showed in that war. Let our language keep you strong and you will never forget what it is to be Navajo. You will never forget what it means to walk in beauty.

# AUTHOR'S NOTE

## Who Are the Navajos?

Before speaking about this novel, I need to say a few words about the history and present circumstances of the Navajos, those who call themselves Dine', a word meaning "The People."

Ethnologists tells us that the distant ancestors of the Navajos came into the Southwest 1,000 or more years ago. That may be so, for their language links them with the Athabaskan people of Alaska. The Navajos themselves say that they emerged into this world from a hole in the earth and that this world is only one of a number they have lived on until catastrophic events forced them to leave.

The place where they arrived is an area bounded by four sacred mountains, now known as the Four Corners area, where the present-day states of New Mexico, Arizona, Colorado, and Utah come together. It is seen by them as a giant house or hogan. The sky is its roof, the earth is its floor, and those mountains are the house poles.

That image alone should be enough to make anyone realize how deeply spiritual and poetic Navajo traditions are. Those traditions appear to be related to those of the Pueblo nations of the Southwest. They include incredibly beautiful chants used in healing ceremonies in which they appeal to the sacred spirits, their "Holy People." Translations into English of some of those chants or "Ways" are today some of the best-known examples of American Indian oral tradition:

Beauty above me I walk
Beauty below me I walk
Beauty behind me I walk
Beauty before me I walk
Beauty all around me I walk
In beauty all is restored
In beauty all is made whole

Some historians have characterized the Navajos as warlike raiders, preying on the other tribes in their region. I do not believe this is accurate, especially when one considers the importance of balance and peace in the sacred ways of the Dine'. The arrival of the Spanish appears to have deeply upset the balance within and between the native nations of the Southwest. The Spanish also introduced widespread slavery. Throughout the Mexican southwest that later became New Mexico, countless thousands of American Indians were captured and forced to work in the mines or as personal slaves. Virtually every Spanish household had its complement of Indian slaves. Navajo resistance to the slave trade was described as raiding by the Spanish.

When the United States gained control of the Southwest, the Navajos thought at first they'd been liberated. Unfortunately, the Americans listened not to the Indians, but to the New Mexicans, who wished to continue the slave trade and convinced the United States to engage in warfare against the Navajos. A brutal campaign was then waged, under the leadership of Kit Carson. It resulted in the total defeat of the Navajos, the destruction of their homes, fields, and orchards, and their forced exile for several years to a bleak outpost in eastern New Mexico, far from Dinetah.

The Navajo Long Walk, which ended that campaign, was as awful an experience for the Navajos as the Trail of Tears was for the Cherokees. It was a forced march of almost the entire Navajo nation. More than 10,000 people trudged 400 miles across mountains and deserts to a desolate Army post. So many died along the way that modern Navajos still speak of it as if it were just yesterday.

By the late 1860s, some thought that the Navajos were not only a defeated people, but a people on their way to extinction. Yet the Navajos never gave up. After years of bitter exile, they were allowed to return to their homeland only after pledging never again to take arms against the United States. Their warrior tradition was supposed to be ended forever.

The recovery of the Najavo nation that took place over the next century and a half is so incredible that one might conclude that not only are the Navajos one of the most remarkable native nations that has ever existed but also that they have truly been blessed and protected by their Holy People. Today, the Navajo Reservation comprises 26,897 square miles. It is the largest Indian reservation in the United States. There are more than 200,000 Navajos. Although it is not without its problems and challenges, the Navajo nation has been described as one of the most economically prosperous and forward-looking of all the American Indian nations in the United States. Yet it is also true that a deep regard remains for the ancient traditions of Dinetah.

## The Code Talkers

I've long been fascinated by the story of the Navajo code talkers and the role they played in World War Two. In that part of the conflict that was fought against Japan in the Pacific Ocean, Navajo Marines used their native language to create an unbreakable code. Because they were Marines, that arm of the U.S. military that leads all others into the thick of battle, they also saw some of the heaviest fighting of the war. If any American servicemen deserved to be honored, it was those Navajos.

But for decades there were no parades, no public honors, no official recognitions of the crucial role they played. From the end of the war in 1945 until 1969, the very existence of a Navajo code and the intelligent and courageous work of those several hundred Navajo Indian Marines remained top secret.

I was born in 1942. Like many others of my generation, World War Two is a part of my own family's history.

Several of my relatives saw intense action in that war, including my aunt Margaret, whose early death was a result of a disease contracted while she was an army nurse in the Philippines. My uncle Jimmy, James Smith Jr., was himself a Marine in the Third Division, Third Tank Battalion, Company B. He took part in such campaigns as Bougainville and Iwo Jima, two places where code talkers played a vital role. The conversations I've had with Uncle Jim about his experiences in the war and the information he shared with me helped me understand what it was like on those grim and distant islands where the Marine Corps was the first to land. Uncle Jim even loaned me such rare volumes as *The Third Marine Division* and *Captain Bryan's Pacific War Atlas*.

My uncle remembered the presence of those Navajo Marines. However, his impression, like that of most other Marines, was that the Navajos were being used as scouts. "I always figured those Indians had some important job," Uncle Jim said. "But it was kept secret from us." He never knew their real story until more than three decades after the end of the war.

Today, despite a number of books and a major Hollywood movie starring Nicolas Cage—as a shell-shocked non-Indian Marine whose personal story takes center stage—the true story of the code talkers still remains relatively unknown. Because of the top secret nature of their role, none of the major books written about World War Two before 1969 contain any mention of them. To this day it's still easy for both historians and the general public to talk and write about the Pacific campaign without feeling the necessity to mention the Navajo code talkers.

That lack of understanding and appreciation is one of the reasons I ended up telling this story. However, I must confess that I never intended to write this book. Somehow, over the last decade, the project took on a life of its own and swept me along with it.

Two things led to my taking on this project. The first was my interest in the American Indian languages. My own tribal heritage is western Abenaki. My family has been deeply involved in trying to preserve and teach this language, which now has a base of less than forty fluent speakers. It is almost that bad for most of the more than 300 indigenous languages that were spoken before Columbus in what is now the United States. The loss of our languages was accelerated by the development in the late nineteenth century of government boarding schools. Virtually all American Indian children were forced into these schools, much like the one my protagonist in this novel attends. In those schools, everything that was Indian was forbidden. Lieutenant Richard Pratt's Carlisle Indian Industrial School in Pennsylvania was the model. Pratt's motto was to "Kill the Indian and save the man." Indian language was a weed to be pulled up by its roots and thrown on the trash heap.

Yet half a century later, boarding school–educated Indians, who'd been told their language and culture were of no use to the modern world, were recruited by the United States and asked to use that language they'd been ordered to forget in the defense of their country. It is one of the greatest ironies of American history that American Indian languages have been of that sort of use to the very nation that forbade them. During World War One, such languages as Cherokee and Choctaw were employed by American Indian soldiers in the trenches to radio messages the Germans couldn't understand. In the European theater of war during World War Two, Comanche Indian soldiers used their language to send similar messages. However, only the Navajo language was used to create a true code—which the Marines used not just in World War Two, but also during the Korean and Vietnam Wars.

Because of my interest in language preservation, those stories of native tongues being used by the military really stuck with me. In some ways, this novel can be read as a parable about the importance of respecting other languages and cultures.

It's even more ironic that Navajos were the Indians chosen by the Marines. Many of those men had grandparents who were survivors of that U.S. Army campaign fought to destroy the Navajos in the 1860s and the nightmarish Long Walk that concluded it.

This brings me to the second thing that led to my taking on this project. In 1996 I was commissioned by the National Geographic Society to research and write a book about the survival of two remarkable American Indian nations. Those nations were the Cherokee and the Navajos, and the eventual book, *Trails of Tears, Paths of Beauty*, was published in 2000.

As I traveled the route of the Navajo Long Walk and

spoke with many different Navajo people, I began to think again about the code talkers' story. Some of the Navajo people I met were code talkers, but it seemed that every Navajo had some connection in one way or another to those brave men. The wartime experience of the code talkers, and what they did when they returned to the United States, turned out to be a major force in shaping the destiny of their people. Code talkers took the lessons they had learned while serving in the military and put them into the service of their people and their culture. Seeing all they did, as teachers, as businessmen, as artists, as major tribal leaders, made me respect them even more.

My first book for the National Geographic Society led to a second one, a picture book entitled *Navajo Long Walk* that I did with my friend Shonto Begay, a Navajo artist whose pictures told the story even more powerfully than my words. So I suggested the idea of another picture book, this time one about the code talkers. When National Geographic Books declined the idea, I took it to another of my publishers, Lee and Low Books. My good friend Philip Lee liked the idea. With his editorial input, I worked through six different drafts. Finally, after more than a year of work, Philip decided it just wasn't working. "This story is too big for a picture book," he told me. I knew he was right.

My next step was to rethink it as a novel and propose it to one of my favorite editors, Lauri Hornik at Dial. She accepted my proposal enthusiastically, even though I know her enthusiasm was dampened—if not drowned—

by the first draft of the book I sent to her. After years of research, reading hundreds of books and countless articles, watching documentary films, visiting museums and libraries, speaking with many people, including surviving code talkers, there was an immense amount of history that I felt needed to be told. As a result, that first full draft was so heavy with facts—names, dates, places—that you could have used it as an anchor.

"Don't worry," I said. "The character will come out more as I revise it. There'll be a little less history and a lot more of his story."

There's still a lot of history in this story and I've done my best to keep it accurate. Even though my main character and narrator is fictitious, I haven't invented events. Everything that happens to Ned Begay happened to real Navajo people, including the boarding school episodes at the start of the tale. With the exception of some of the white Marines, such as his buddies Smitty and Georgia Boy, the characters named in this novel are all real people. Their stories have been well-documented elsewhere.

Whatever I have done, however, this is not my story. It belongs to the Navajo people. Anything that is good in it must be credited to them. I thank them for it. And though I've tried to do my best, I know that I am only a human being and that I may have made mistakes. For that I am truly sorry. However, I believe that the beauty and power of the Navajo Way is so great that it will shine through whatever clouds of confusion my own failings may have created. The lessons my Navajo friends have shared with me over the years are truly the only reason I was able to attempt this inspiring, important story, a tale that is as much about the beauty of peace and understanding as it is about the pain and confusion of war.

# SELECTED BIBLIOGRAPHY

## Books About the Navajos

Acrey, Bill P. *Navajo History, The Land and the People.* Shiprock, N.M.: Department of Curriculum Materials Development, 1978.

Aronilth, Wilson. *Foundation of Navajo Culture.* "Navajoland, USA," (no publisher listed) 1992.

Bulow, Ernie. *Navajo Taboos.* Gallup, N.M.: Buffalo Medicine Books, 1991.

Callaway, Sydney M. and others. *Grandfather Stories of the Navajos.* Chinle, AZ: Rough Rock Press, 1974

Iverson, Porter. *The Navajos.* New York, Chelsea House Publishers, 1990.

Locke, Raymond Friday. *The Book of the Navajo.* Los Angeles, CA: Mankind Publishing, 1976, 1992.

Mitchell, Frank (edited by Charlotte F. Frisbie and David P. McAllester). *Navajo Blessingway Singer, The Autobiography of Frank Mitchell, 1881-1967.* Tucson, AZ: University of Arizona Press, 1978.

Rock Point Community School. *Between Sacred Mountains.* Tucson, AZ: Sun Tracks and the University of Arizona Press, 1982

Roessel, Ruth (compiler). *Navajo Stories of the Long Walk Period.* Tsaile, Navajo Nation, AZ: Navajo Community College Press, 1973

Thompson, Hildegard. *The Navajos' Long Walk for Education.* Tsaile, AZ: Navajo Community College Press, 1975

Young, Robert W., and William Morgan. *Colloquial Navajo, A Dictionary.* New York: Hippocrene Books, 1994 (originally compiled in 1951 for U.S. Indian Service).

# Books About the Code Talkers

Aaseng, Nathan. *Navajo Code Talkers, America's Secret Weapon in World War II.* New York: Walker & Company, 1992.

Bixtler, Margaret T. *Winds of Freedom, The Story of the Navajo Code Talkers of World War II.* Darien, CT: Two Bytes Publishing, 1992.

Durrett, Deane. *Unsung Heroes of World War II: The Story of the Navajo Code Talkers.* New York: Facts on File, 1998.

Greenburg, Henry, and Georgia Greenburg. *Power of a Navajo, Carl Gorman: The Man and his Life.* Santa Fe, N.M.: Clear Light Publishers, 1996.

Kawano, Kenji. *Warriors: Navajo Code Talkers.* Tucson, AZ: Northland, 1990.

McClain, Sally. *Navajo Weapon.* Tucson, AZ: Rio Nuevo Publishers, 2001.

Paul, Doris A. *The Navajo Code Talkers.* Pittsburgh: Dorrance Publishing Company, 1973.

# Books About World War Two

Anderson, Christopher A. *The Marines in World War II, From Pearl Harbor to Tokyo Bay.* London, U.K.: Greenhill Books, 2000

Gailey, Harry A. *The War in the Pacific, From Pearl Harbor to Tokyo Bay.* Novato, CA: Presidio Press, 1995.

Jowett, Phillip. *The Japanese Army 1931-1945* (2 volumes). Oxford, U.K.: Osprey Publishing Inc, 2002.

Leckie, Robert. *Okinawa, The Last Battle of World War II.* New York: Penguin Books, 1995.

Moran, Jim, and Gordon L. Rottman. *Pelelieu 1944, The Forgotten Corner of Hell.* Oxford, U.K.: Osprey Publishing, 2002.

Newcomb, Robert F. *Iwo Jima.* New York: Henry Holt & Co., 1965.

Rottman, Gordon L. *Okinawa, The Last Battle.* Oxford, U.K.: Osprey Publishing Inc, 2002.

Tregaskis, Richard. *Guadalcanal Diary.* New York: The Modern Library, 2000 (updated reissue of the Random House, 1943 edition).

Wright, Derrick. *Iwo Jima, 1945, The Marines Raise the Flag on Mount Suribachi.* Oxford, U.K.: Osprey Publishing, 2001.

Wright, Derrick. *Tarawa 1943, The Turning of the Tide.* Oxford, U.K.: Osprey Publishing, 2000.

# ACKNOWLEDGMENTS

First of all, I want to express my gratitude to the Navajo nation in general. Whenever I have visited Dinetah, I have always been treated by the Navajo people with such patient grace and good humor that it has made me feel as if I was a welcome guest. I wish I could list everyone by name who has helped and taught me over the years, but there's not enough space. Here are the names of those people I must mention.

Thanks to Shonto Begay, Rex Lee Jim, and Wilson Hunter for what you've taught me through your work and our all-too-brief conversations. Many thanks to Nia Francisco, Luci Tapahonso, and Laura Tohe, three Navajo women who are also among our country's finest poets. Your work has meant a great deal to me over the last two decades, inspiring and informing me, just as you have done for countless readers.

For this story in particular, I have to say a very big thanks to Keith Little, current secretary of the Navajo Code Talkers Association. It was my very good fortune to have been invited, along with Mr. Little and Jesse Samuel Smith, to tell stories at the Smithsonian Tent during the first National Book Fair in Washington, D.C. Not only did I get a chance to hear them speak about their experiences as code talkers, I was able to hang around with them, hear some more tales, and share some very funny experiences, including a memorable breakfast at the White House. The further information about the experience of being a Navajo Marine during World War Two that Mr. Little was kind enough to share with me in response to my letters and phone calls was incredibly valuable.

Mention of Washington, D.C., brings to mind those institutions whose archives are true national treasures—the Library of Congress and the Smithsonian Institution. Without the work they have done to preserve the knowledge that empowers us all, I would not have been able to write this story. It is impossible for me to express how grateful I am for the existence of one branch of the Smithsonian, in particular—the National Museum of the American Indian (NMAI). NMAI, with its three branches in Suitland, Maryland, New York City, and Washington, D.C., is not only the greatest repository of information about our many native nations, it is also a dynamic force in maintaining and renewing American Indian culture.

It was at the New York City branch of NMAI that I met Carl Gorman for the first time in 1996. Mr. Gorman had long been one of my personal heroes for his inspiring work as an artist. However, I had not known until then the important role he played in 1942 when he was, at thirty-five, the oldest man in that first group of twenty-nine Navajo recruits who developed the code. I also met his daughter, Zonnie Gorman, who screened the still-incomplete film she was making about the code talkers. Since her father passed on, she has continued to be active as a speaker, sharing her father's legacy and the code talkers' stories. I hope she will find the support and time to complete that film.

Whenever I write or say anything about Dine' culture I would be deeply remiss if I failed to mention Harry Walters, Navajo culture teacher and director of the Hathathli Museum at Dine' College. Thank you for your committed brilliance and your careful, compassionate scholarship, Harry. You are an inspiration to all of us who believe in preserving the language, the stories, and the ways of our ancestors.